S.T.A.R.S. sixth formers are taking part in a French exchange with a Parisian school. What will their partners be like? Colette is worried – she has to share a room with hers. And what will they show them? As it turns out, the French want to see a piece of the action, and Dim is the only one who can give them a good time. At least it's something to boost his ego. After all, Colette doesn't want commitment and isn't that a rejection of his chunky charms?

Once in Paris, Colette thinks her French family are really odd. Do they have a madman locked in the attic? Raffy has his eye on the beautiful Blanche, but thinks he needs protecting from an older woman. Perhaps he'd be safer in the *lycée* than staying with his exchange. And *is* there a connection between the French exchange teacher and S.T.A.R.S.' new campaign?

This is the ninth book in the S.T.A.R.S. sequence. Every month there is a new, self-contained story, all about the same group of sixth formers. S.T.A.R.S. is based on reality, taking you inside a modern London comprehensive. It's funny, action-packed and full of great characters. Join now. The common-room door is always open. Waiting for you . . .

Hunter Davies is an author, journalist and broadcaster. He has written over thirty books, ranging from biographies of the Beatles to William Wordsworth, and he wrote the 'Father's Day' column in *Punch* for ten years. He is the author of the *Flossie Teacake* stories and has also written a book for teenagers, *Saturday Night*. He has three children and lives in London.

HUNTER DAVIES

PENGUIN BOOKS

PENGUIN BOOKS

Published by the Penguin Group
27 Wrights Lane, London W8 5TZ, England
Viking Penguin Inc., 40 West 23rd Street, New York, New York 10010, USA
Penguin Books Australia Ltd, Ringwood, Victoria, Australia
Penguin Books Canada Ltd, 2801 John Street, Markham, Ontario,
Canada L3R 1B4
Penguin Books (NZ) Ltd, 182–190 Wairau Road, Auckland 10, New Zealand

Penguin Books Ltd, Registered Offices: Harmondsworth, Middlesex, England

First published 1990
1 3 5 7 9 10 8 6 4 2

Filmset in Linotron Ehrhardt by
Rowland Phototypesetting Ltd,
Bury St Edmunds, Suffolk
Printed and bound in Great Britain by
Cox and Wyman Ltd, Reading, Berks.

Dim: big and chunky

EPISODE 1

Outside St Andrews Road
School, Monday

Another hard day is over. If it's Monday, it's bound
to have been hard. Just getting up and off to school,
that's bad enough. For those who slept in and
arrived late – which, alas, often happens on a
Monday – little has been gained. Not when there's a
whole week stretching ahead like a lifetime. Even
in the sixth form, Mondays are a drag, despite
the privilege, nay, the luxury, of having a certain
number of free periods. Mondays are Moandays.

But spring has come to St Andrews Road at last,
with the weather to prove it. In the school garden,
that narrow stretch of brave lawn and hopeful trees
behind the Old and New Buildings, saved for the
nation from the combined ravages of concrete,
graffiti and a thousand pairs of heavy feet, birds are

5

singing and flowers are fluttering. In the main road outside, there are also spring-like noises. Cars are singing. Drivers are fluttering. The unexpected sunshine has made them open up their windows and sunroofs. In-car stereos are providing out-car entertainment, turned up to full volume, with every speaker now speaking to the world at large.

Inside school, quite a few minds are tuning themselves into spring. Many a young person's fancy is already idly turning to thoughts of, well, fancying. More especially that select band of lower sixth formers who have something special to look forward to this spring. Some new sounds perhaps, from a new station.

'Can I see you home?' asks Dim, wheeling his bike down the main drive towards the front gates.

The bell has just gone and to his surprise, Colette has raced off, straight out of the common room, hardly stopping to kiss her fond goodbyes to Ella and Kirsty. They do this every day after school, even if they are going to meet again in half an hour.

'Depends how good your eyes are,' says Colette.

'You what?' says Dim, trying to keep abreast of Colette while pushing kids out of the way of his bike. Being so big, so chunky, he hardly has to use force. Most sensible people will steer clear, but he doesn't want any stray nasty hands or feet touching his precious machine.

'No, thanks,' says Colette. 'I am capable of finding my own way home. I left chalk marks this morning.'

'Well, I just thought –' begins Dim.

'Don't,' says Colette. 'It can be dangerous. Keep all your thoughts for Maths.'

'What you got on tonight?'

'Clothes, probably,' says Colette. 'I find sitting naked to do my essay a bit uncomfortable.'

'I'd like to see that,' says Dim, trying to summon up a leer but not managing it very well. Leering is not in his character.

'You sound like Raffy.'

'He says he's seeing you tonight,' says Dim.

'Then it must be true,' says Colette. 'Raffy would never lie, would he?'

'What are you seeing him for?' asks Dim.

'Look, Dim, I've got to rush. See you tomorrow.'

Colette dashes down a lane, a short cut towards her street, giving Dim a final wave. She has nothing against him. But on reflection, after due consideration, she can't honestly think of a great many things going in favour of him.

She looks at her watch and groans aloud. Women don't run, she thinks, just as women don't sweat, but this is urgent. She'll have to break one of her own rules, however undignified the result. She'd better hurry if she wants to get home before her mother.

Colette's flat

'Hi, Mum,' shouts Colette, opening the door of her flat. She presumes, and hopes, that her mother will not yet be in, so her shout is simply to clear the air, clear her lungs, clear out any afternoon burglars who might be lurking about.

7

She sniffs, taking in that familiar late-afternoon smell, her coming-home-to-an-empty-home smell. A combination of stale, dead air, last night's supper and some mint-fresh gas. They have a leak somewhere, from the gas heater, they think, but it's not serious enough to worry or complain to the landlord about. Colette has taken in this mixture every day after school for years. She thinks it will always be in her nostrils, wherever she ends up living.

As ever, the smells slowly and subtly fade, just as soon as a living breathing human being moves into the space, stirs up a bit of life, gets the evening show on the road, creating another atmosphere. It's only in those first few moments that Colette can pick up the smells of home, not-so-sweet home. Even the whiff of gas quickly disappears, which is why they never do anything about it.

Colette goes first to the fridge to see what goodies her mother has left her, some little soupçon to keep her alive till supper, or the next little soupçon.

'Hurrah, she's done what I told her to do for once. She's not a bad old cow.'

She has found two chocolate-covered croissants, carefully placed between two plates. Her fingers are into one of them at once, checking the state of the chocolate topping, the quality of the filling. She stands and contemplates. In her head, she is fighting two battles with herself. She tries to look ahead and forecast the outcome. Believing in free will, she knows this outcome is still in doubt. Until she makes up her mind, or it gets made up for her, she doesn't know which way she'll go. Whether she'll win both battles. Or neither.

Colette prefers her croissants hot, always has done. That's just the sort of gel she is. God willed it that way. When you have your croissants hot, the chocolate goes beautifully runny on top, the filling gorgeously gooey inside, and the dough turns succulent and fragrant. Yum, yum. But can she wait, can she deny her taste-buds, can she withhold the pleasure a moment longer? She dearly wants to guzzle now, not delay fifteen minutes while the oven heats up.

'If only we had a micro, like Kirsty. It's not fair, I keep telling the old bat. I am a deprived child.'

She lights the oven and puts in one of the croissants, turning the gas up high.

'Steady, old girl,' she tells herself. '*Doucement, doucement.* Hey, that's good. Sweetness and soft-ness, all in the same word. Just what I want. The old Frog language can be quite useful.'

Colette stands and waits. And that's when she loses the second battle, her impatience getting the better of her. She knows the other croissant is for her mother. That's the custom, share and share alike. They each have an equally sweet tooth, so they split the goodies and help each other. After all, who else have they got.

The fridge door opens again, almost, but not quite, on its own. A hand goes in, almost, but not quite, a ghost-like hand, because there's a flesh and blood mouth at the end of it. And into this mouth, very quickly, goes the second, cold, croissant.

Gobble, gobble, lick, lick, down it jolly well goes. Colette wets her fingers to gather up any crumbs, then uses her tongue for the final flakings. She's just in time for the first croissant to come out of the oven, all hot and yummy.

Colette's mother's bedroom

Colette is listening hard. Her mother's bedroom door is open, so she can hear any steps coming up the stairs outside, see any movement of the front-door handle of their little flat. She throws open her mother's wardrobe door and starts searching, forcing clothes to one side, pushing them into corners, yanking them out to have a better look, then shaking her head, putting them back in again. Or not. Some she has to lay on the bed. The wardrobe is so jam-packed that some outfits, once removed, won't go back in place again.

Colette curses as various wire coat-hangers take on a life of their own, intertwining like ivy, refusing to be parted. Whole batches of dresses have to be dragged out, pulling their friends with them, when she only wants to look at one. Getting them back in the wardrobe leads to further oaths. The coat-hangers have somehow rearranged themselves, out of spite, facing different ways, so they can't be returned in a single batch, but have to be forcibly separated and put back one by one.

'All horrible, absolutely horrible. Where the hell does she get such junk from.'

She goes to a chest of drawers, rifling through each drawer in turn, dragging things out, then stuffing them back in again. Her mother keeps all her belongings in such a state that Colette has no qualms about shoving things back in a different order. Her mother will never tell.

At last, she finds some black tights. Rather heavy for a warm spring evening, but this is the pair Colette has been looking for. She gives the feet a quick sniff, just in case, not that it will matter either way. She has found the first item she has been searching for.

In the dirty laundry basket she finds the second item, a white silk blouse. She holds it up. Yes, there is a wine stain, but low down. Who will see it if it's worn with the third item, the most important thing she's searching for. She puts the blouse on a hanger. The worst of the creases might come out in an hour, before the outfit goes on show and stuns the world.

'Oh God, where is it?' moans Colette, looking in the wardrobe once again, on the floor amidst various fallen pieces of clothing, and on the shelf above. 'Don't say she's got it on for work. No, she wouldn't. Not today.'

She looks under the bed, just in case, shoving her hand around in the hope of making some discovery. She pulls out her mother's pink tracksuit, all scrunched up.

'Typical. That's the way she looks after all her things.'

Colette holds the tracksuit at arm's length. Not because it's dirty, but because the colour and the size, the style and the texture, totally offend her.

11

'Yuck,' she exclaims, dropping it into the laundry basket and closing the lid. 'How can she even sleep with it under her bed.'

Colette thinks she hears a noise. She stands still, waiting. Two lots of footsteps can be heard going upstairs. But they pass, straight on up. It must be the primary-school teacher in the flat above. Bringing someone home, perhaps, someone she doesn't want made public, judging by the lack of conversation. She goes to open the bedroom door even wider. And there it is, hanging on the hook under two dressing gowns. No wonder she never saw it earlier. How lucky that the merest flash of brown caught her eye.

It is a suede suit. Dark brown and nicely tailored, with neat shoulders, not too pronounced, well-cut lapels, not too wide, and a straight skirt, but not too tarty. Her mother doesn't like the outfit, as she thinks it makes her look like a health visitor. Not that she, or Colette, knows what a health visitor dresses like.

'Right, that's it,' says Colette, clearing up the odd clothes she has failed to hang up or stow away, and shoving them under the bed. She then lays out the tights, the blouse and the suit neatly on the bed. She locks the wardrobe and puts the key in the top drawer of the chest of drawers, jamming all the other drawers tightly closed.

'If she still insists on coming with me, then this is it. My condition. She wears these, or else. I don't want her looking like a tramp all her life. Especially not in front of my friends.'

Taz: deeply embarrassed

EPISODE 2

Inside school, later that
Monday evening

Liz Ainley, Head of French, is addressing a select group of parents and students. She had hoped for many more, perhaps thirty people at most, which is why she decided to have her little *soirée* in the Old Hall, rather than the French department. It's an informal get-together, nothing too rigid. She wants everyone to be friends, which is why she has handed round peanuts and glasses of French red wine, goodish quality, out of her own pocket. No one presumes this has been paid for from her teacher's salary. She is said to have a wealthy lawyer husband, though she never talks about him.

Everyone is sitting in a circle, on rather hard

chairs, at one end of the hall just under the stage. From a distance, they look lost, cowering like refugees. The school caretaker has not put all the lights on as it's such a small gathering, which makes the hall seem even eerier.

'I just wanted to tell you personally that, over the years, we've had great success with this *lycée*. In fact, we're now exchanging the younger brothers and sisters of students who visited us in the past . . .'

Mrs Ainley has a very strong Lancashire accent. The students are no longer aware of it, but one or two parents are exchanging glances. She is large and plump and goes in for leather boots, very short skirts and jazzy tights, which are often not in perfect condition. Most of the students like her, though she and Colette have had their ups and downs. In the first year, some kids did snigger at her appearance, but they soon found out she had a quick temper, was very keen on discipline and made people work as hard as she did herself.

'Some of you might have gone on the fourth-year French trip to Abbeville, but, as you know, that is mainly a holiday, an introductory experience. In the lower sixth, we have a proper exchange on a much smaller scale, rather exclusive, so I like to think. And I like to look upon it as work, as a valuable experience for all those doing A-level French. That's who it is aimed at, though over the years we have had exchanges between people in the lower sixth who are no longer taking French . . .'

Colette looks around at the listening faces. Only eight lower-sixth pupils have turned up, out of the ten who originally said they were interested. Each was supposed to have brought along his or her parents or guardians. Only eight of these have turned up. She glances at her mother. Quite a credit, really, when she thinks what a mess she usually is. Mind you, compared with Mrs Ainley, even her mother would look passable. She only hopes her mother remembers the second instruction for the evening. Which was to keep her gob shut.

Colette then quietly observes Taz's father. He looks smart and city-like, in a pinstripe suit and a red shirt with a white collar, but he is small and balding and he will fidget. He keeps looking at his watch, then beaming around the room, proprietorially, as if it's his meeting, his hall, perhaps even his school.

Jules is with his father, though trying hard to pretend he's not. Poor Jules, thinks Colette. His father is wearing trainers, a leather bomber jacket and a holey pullover, yet he must be all of forty, and very well-off too. He is obviously bored, sighing heavily from time to time. Still, he has made an effort to turn up, which makes a change – Jules doesn't usually see very much of him.

The other parents are more cowed. They are in their best going-out clothes, sitting stiffly, some looking worried, as if finding it hard to follow what is happening.

'The plan is very simple,' continues Mrs Ainley. 'Their students will have five days at our school, going to our lessons, then our students will go to

Paris for five days, attending their school and their lessons.'

'Oh Gawd,' says Raffy. 'So it is work. Bloody hell, Lizzie. I thought it was gonna be a laugh. I'm not going if it's work.'

Raffy is sitting on his own, parentless. He has not told his grandmother, with whom he lives, about this meeting or the possible Paris trip. He has spent most of the evening so far finishing off the wine in any unclaimed glasses he can find. Several parents stare at him, not sure if he is a member of staff. Surely no student would address a teacher in such an over-familiar manner.

'Well, I hope you will come, Raffy,' says Mrs Ainley. 'I know you are so gifted at French that you might not learn as much as some other people, but I'm sure we'd all be much better for your company. As would Paris.'

At the mention of his name, a few parents turn discreetly to look at him. So that's Raffy. That's the one they've heard tales about all these years. He's smaller than some imagined, but he does look very Raffy-ish. The ones with daughters wonder if it's too late for a private school.

'So what's the cost going to be, then?' asks Raffy.

'Well, I've not got exact prices yet, but last year we did it all-in for £45 each. That covers the cost of transport, travel insurance and various excursions for the French students when they are with us, for which we pay. They pay for us there. This year I hope it will be no more than £50 per head. That doesn't include pocket money, of course. Any other queries?'

'I'd like to thank Mrs Hanley,' says Taz's father, standing up and beaming round, 'on behalf of us all, for the great job she is doing. And I'd just like to ask one question. What about accommodation in Paris? I do have various contacts in the hotel trade and I'm sure –'

The loud buzz of a telephone makes everyone jump, including Taz's father. He takes out a mobile phone from his pocket, looking not at all embarrassed. He does at least have the courtesy to go off into a corner to answer it. Everyone laughs. Taz wants to crawl under the floorboards. That was the final thing she said to him. Don't wear that con-man's shirt and on no account bring the stupid phone.

'Perhaps I haven't made it clear,' says Mrs Ainley. 'It's an exchange. If ten of you decide to go, then ten French pupils will come here. They will stay at your homes, here in London, and you will stay in their homes in Paris.

'Anyway, it's all made clear in these forms here. I want you to fill them in, return them to me, then we can start matching students. Please pass them round.'

Raffy jumps up without taking any forms, his face set. 'That's it, then,' he thinks to himself. 'I haven't got the money, and I can't have anyone back to my place. What a waste of time.'

Colette is also looking worried. She hadn't thought of this either. How can she possibly

put someone up in their little flat, with her
mother?

Raffy is already across the hall, heading for the
door. Mrs Ainley brings the meeting to an end,
telling everyone to contact her about any queries
and to return the forms as quickly as possible.

The Cow and Bull, half an hour later

Sam and Ella are sitting together, legs touching and
sometimes hands. They were having such a quiet,
peaceful, non-alcoholic drink together, till the world
and his offspring barged in. Now, there's quite a
little gang.

First came Raffy, all bad-tempered. Followed by
Colette, equally irritable. It was a struggle to shake
off her mother, but she managed to send her home
on her own by saying she had a date with Dim.
Which was a lie. Dim is the last person she wants to
see. The next person to arrive was Dim himself,
hoping to see Colette, which immediately made her
even more irritable. Finally, Toby appeared, knowing he was bound to find some of his friends here,
even on a Monday evening, when all good people
should be at their studies or saving their pennies.

'What about your parents, Sam?' asks Ella. 'They
could help Raffy.'

'You mean, take him in and wash him?' says Sam.
Raffy gives him a push which sends Sam sprawling
on the floor.

'Neville,' shouts Raffy, 'get this drunk out of
here. I thought you didn't allow rubbish on your
new carpet.'

'I mean you've got a spare bedroom,' says Ella. 'Your mother is always so welcoming. That would solve one of Raffy's problems. You could easily put up a French boy for five days, just to help Raffy out.'

'Yeah,' says Sam. 'I'll ask her.'

Colette is saying nothing on this subject. She has already had words with her mother at the school gates. Her mother will insist that they have bags of room in their flat, lashings of space. What's the problem? We can all muck in together, and what a help it will be for Colette, having a mother who got O-level French.

'Or how about you, Toby?' says Ella. 'You've got a big house.'

'That is true,' says Toby. 'But it's full of lodgers. My parents are so mean they'd probably charge.'

'I bet Taz has bags of room,' says Raffy. 'I know, me and some frog can both go and stay at her place.'

'Where is she, anyway?' asks Dim.

'She went straight off home with her dad,' says Colette.

'No wonder,' says Raffy. 'Who wants to pig it in this dump. Same old people, same old lousy beer – are you listening, Neville? Okay, I will have another one, Toby. As you're paying. It is your round, I bought them all before you came.'

'What a lie,' says Ella.

'I was really looking forward to this trip,' says Raffy. 'Anything to get out of boring old school. And get out of boring old London. Get shacked up with a few little Parisian mademoiselles.'

'If you go, could you write a bit for the magazine?' says Toby.

'If I go, I'll do you a serial story,' says Raffy. 'Before, during and after, with saucy photographs. But it's not even worth filling in that stupid form she was handing out unless I can get the dosh and find somewhere for my exchange to stay.'

'I've told you,' says Sam, getting up, followed by Ella, both ready to depart. 'I'll ask the wrinklies.'

'Thanks,' says Raffy. 'Hey, it's that way. Into the lavatory, first on the right. Have you got enough change? Ha ha. Always be prepared you know, ha ha.'

Raffy is shouting, just to embarrass Sam and Ella. Colette is shushing him, telling him to keep quiet.

'If it's working, mind you. Not you, Sam, I know you're in full working order, ha ha. I've seen the evidence. Ha ha. I mean the machine. It's usually bust in this place.'

'You are a fool, Raffy,' says Colette when Sam and Ella have finally gone. 'That wasn't funny, you know.'

'I was being deadly serious, actually,' says Raffy. 'Look, the Government has spent millions telling teenagers to be prepared, so I'm just helping, ain't I.'

'No, you weren't,' says Toby. 'You were being smutty.'

'Oh, hark at him,' says Raffy. 'Smutty, huh? Look, just go into those bogs and you'll see. Every Gents in the land has those machines, and most are vandalized. This one always is.'

'Probably by you,' says Colette. 'We know your sort.'

'Now who's being stupid and smutty,' says Raffy.

'You,' says Dim, trying to take Colette's side, hoping to be her ally, if not her close friend. She ignores him.

'Tell you what should be done, Toby,' continues Raffy, warming to a new theme which he's just thought of. 'As you are on the Sixth-Form Committee, here's an idea for free. We should have *our* own machines, in *our* sixth-form lavatories. Wouldn't that be a good idea, huh?'

'Stupid, really stupid, if you ask me,' says Colette, getting up. Dim rises as well, ready to follow her out, determined to accompany her home whatever she says, as it is dark.

But Dim has registered the possibilities of Raffy's suggestion. And so has Toby, though in somewhat more of a philosophical than a financial sense.

Kirsty: laughing at Raffy

EPISODE 3

ST ANDREWS ROAD SCHOOL:
FRENCH EXCHANGE
The following details will help us pair you
with a French boy/girl. Please fill in and ask
your parent or guardian to complete and sign
in the appropriate place. Then return to me as
soon as possible. Thank you.

E. Ainley

Name of student: *Raffy, BA, BBC, SOS, SEX*
Tutor group: *Boring old Grotty's*
Hobbies and interests (please give as much detail
as possible):
*Are you serious? There are still laws against libel,
slander, arson and blasphemy, you know. Right,
well, my interests are broad and wide-ranging. I
like to look for broads, and my range is wide. Boom
boom. Yes, girls are my first interest. When I'm not
looking at them, I'm looking for them, when I can't
find them, I'm thinking about them, and when I'm
not thinking about them, I'm unconscious.*

*Now for hobbies. Girls. Sorry, Lizzie my love. I
can't think of any more pastimes. Stamps? Para-
chuting? Too exciting. I'll stick to something more
down to earth, which is how I like them. Oops, just
slipped out. Oops, another slip. What have I said?
'Scuse my French. 'Oops' is French, isn't it? As in
oops alors. Gosh, I'm exhausted already – all this
brainpower. I find thinking is so tiring. Now doing,
being on the job, getting down to it, that is energy-
giving, I always find. Don't you? Give as much
detail as possible? What sort of jerk are you? A dirty
old man, or woman, as the case may be. You
probably want photographs as well, diagrams, in-
side-leg measurements. Sorry, but life is too short
to go into further details – anyway, how long have
you got?*

*I'm also interested in Arsenal, as any intellectual
would be. I do have a sneaking admiration for
another North London football team, which I also
sometimes watch: Arsenal Reserves.*

I like: fillet steak, hamburgers, McDonald's french fries but not their fish things, Taz, the Town and Country Club, Dingwalls, any girls who are nice to me, my gran as she's bound to read this — oh, and Mrs Ainley. I think she's trif and bound to be a goer. Having baths, Taz, Heathcliff, my reflection in a mirror looking from the right, cappuccino, *William Makepeace Thackeray, Marine Ices' chocolate ice cream but not their strawberry, Mrs Thatcher, waking up and realizing it's Saturday, getting paid, getting laid. That must be enough, surely.*

I hate: Spurs, left-wingers, right-wingers, Mondays, getting out of bed, going to bed, waiting for the 24 bus, girls who say no, liver, the way my hair starts curling at the back when it needs washing, Top of the Pops, *anyone who has a perm,* Neighbours, *Holden Caulfield, Kentish Town Swimming Pool, boxer shorts, Tom Stoppard, not managing it when I thought I was on to a winner.*

Any brothers or sisters living at home: *Nope. Searched everywhere but found none so far, unless they're crouching.*

Pets: *Just one. My gran.*

Will your exchange-partner share a room? *Not just a room, they'll share a bed, you wally. Perhaps even the sheets.*

To be filled in by parent or guardian:

1   Are there any medical conditions, allergies or problems we should know about?

Cheeky sod. Why not ask me that? Would I lie? You know me, I don't mind admitting anything. On the medical side, I often have fits, when girls say no or the chips have run out. I am allergic to buttons, great rows of them, the sort which take hours to undo. As for problems, I think you already know about my two wives and three children. That was all way back in the third year, I can hardly remember them myself. But I s'pose I had better mention something new in my life – to wit, a rather nasty wart on my right testicle. (This is confidential, innit? I don't want everyone knowing, especially not the halfwits who have nothing better to do than read the sixth-form magazine.)

2   Please give a brief description of the type of student who is most likely to get on well with your son/daughter (e.g. someone quiet or extrovert, sporting or non-sporting, etc).

   Oh, someone sporting. I.e. a good sport who will laugh at all Raffy's jokes and take her clothes off when told, or even before being told.

Signed:
Student : **Raffy** (in his absence, as he's occupied)

Parent : **Gran** *(her mark, and she'd better clear it up)*

Sixth-form common room, one week later

The latest edition of *Sixth Censored* has just come out. People are sitting around reading it, deliberately pretending not to have noticed Raffy's contribution. Not in front of him, anyway.

'Typical Raffy, puerile,' says Colette.

'Actually,' says Kirsty, 'I think it's funny.'

'Shurrup, you fish. Here he comes.'

Raffy walks straight past and heads for Taz, who is reading in a corner. 'I've decided that you and I together should be the French editors.'

'How kind,' says Taz. 'I'm flattered.'

'No, really. You did that good bit about Mrs Potter in the first magazine. It was you, wasn't it?'

'Might have been.'

'Anyway, if I go on this trip, I thought we could share a French letter . . .'

Taz turns away as Raffy bursts out laughing at his own wit. She should have realized he was leading up to something. But there is a smile on her face.

'Talking about French letters,' says Raffy, going over to where Ella, Toby and Dim are sitting, 'isn't everyone doing just that?'

The three of them are deep in conversation, looking very busy and pleased with themselves.

'So how's it going, then?' asks Raffy.

'Fine, fine,' says Ella. 'We've got the Sixth-Form Committee meeting this evening, after school. We're going to bring it up and make them vote.'

'Can you manage it, Raffy?' asks Toby.

'Any time, squire,' says Raffy.

'I mean the meeting,' says Toby.

'As an observer of course,' says Ella, ignoring Raffy's remark. 'You can't actually vote at the meeting, but your presence would give us moral support.'

'What's wrong with Sam?' says Raffy. 'Or does he just give you immoral support, ha ha.'

Ella blushes. One of the reasons why she has become so involved in this new campaign is that for a short, but very worrying, spell, she feared she had become a victim of the sin of not being prepared and protected.

Colette and Kirsty walk over, followed by Jules, also wanting to know how the new campaign is going.

'It's fifty-fifty,' says Toby. 'Whether we can swing the meeting or not. We're trying for condom machines in both lavatories, boys and girls, but we're willing to give in on one.'

'Gosh, you're all so devious,' says Jules. 'You could easily be politicians. Personally, the sort of machines I want in the bogs are for shoe cleaning. Failing that, a launderette. I think that would be really useful. One can get frightfully dusty, especially in the Old Building. It would be jolly handy to have somewhere fresh and clean to change at lunchtime.'

Jules is sending himself up, but he means some of what he says, as they are all aware. He can see no reason for condom machines anywhere on school premises.

'That might be the sort of thing we'll be asked, Ella,' says Toby. 'Whether other machines wouldn't be more useful.'

'Then the answer is simple,' says Ella. 'We're not just providing a functional facility, like a phone or a stamp machine. Having a condom dispenser is that, but it's also a symbol, a message to the rest of the school to be wise, to be sensible.'

'To be promiscuous, you mean,' says Jules.

'Now why do you take it that way?' says Toby. 'Because things exist, it doesn't mean they have to be used. You get cigarette machines everywhere, but no one ever says the machines are an incitement to smoke. They won't make non-smokers smoke. Just as condom machines won't make people – er – you know, use them.'

'Now take it carefully, Toby old son,' says Raffy. 'We don't want any Anglo-Saxon four-letter words coming out of those rosebud lips at the Committee meeting.'

'And look at pubs,' continues Toby.

'I do constantly,' says Raffy.

'Pubs are open to anyone, but no one accuses them of turning people into alcoholics.'

'Some people do,' says Ella.

'Chocolate machines,' says Toby. 'You see them in railway stations, outside shops, everywhere. If you gorged yourself on chocolate –'

'Oooh, lovely,' says Colette. Dim gives her a big smile. Colette ignores him.

'– If you gorged yourself on chocolate,' continues Toby, 'you could do yourself terrible damage.'

'Oooh, lovely,' says Colette.

'Toby is right,' says Ella. 'A condom dispenser is no different from any other machine. Think about it. It's a facility. We're not making a moral judgement, that's up to the consumer. And our consumers will all be over sixteen, as they're all sixth formers. No laws are being broken. We are all above the age of consent. The Government decreed that age, not us. So what are we doing that is wrong, legally or morally? Tell me.'

'What we are doing is simple,' says Toby, taking up her point, almost as if they have rehearsed this dialogue, which in fact they have. 'We're providing a service, one which happens to be sensible, wouldn't you admit? A health-giving service, wouldn't you agree, compared with doling out cigarettes or chocolates?'

There is silence. Ella and Toby have put their case very succinctly. Kirsty, who up to now thought the whole thing was silly, and Raffy, who thought it was just a joke, are beginning to agree this might be a worthwhile campaign. Even though they personally will not get up the energy to actively help it along.

'So what part are you playing in all this, Dim old son?' asks Raffy, feeling Dim's collar, fingering his suit lapel.

'Watch the material,' grunts Dim. 'After school, I'm off to a pretty important business meeting. While Ella and Toby argue their points, I'll be looking into one or two other aspects which could affect us all . . .'

Fred's Caff, later that evening

Raffy, Jules, Kirsty and Colette are sitting drinking tea, their third cups. There is still no sign of Ella and Toby or of Dim, all three of whom they are very keen to see. Nor Sam, who said he would be here as well.

'I won't be able to go to Paris, anyway,' says Raffy. 'Even if Sam can give a bed to my Frog.'

'Course you can, Raf,' says Colette. 'You've got to. It won't be any fun without you.'

'That's true,' says Raffy. 'But I really haven't got enough dosh. My gran's got bugger-all. I don't get any pocket money, not like you two. It takes all my Saturday-morning earnings just to buy my own clothes and books and stuff.'

'Isn't there a council scheme for poor people?' asks Kirsty.

'Do you mind,' says Raffy.

'No, hold on,' says Kirsty. 'When I was at primary school, I got free dinners and free trips and everything. My dad was on the dole at the time. This was before my brothers went out to work.'

'Now you're on the gravy train, don't tell me,' says Raffy.

'All I'm saying is, there's nothing to be ashamed of,' says Kirsty. 'Not in taking money from the state.'

'You pay for it in the end,' says Colette, 'cos it all comes out of our taxes. It's your money, your right.'

'You tell that to me gran. She won't apply for anything. She thinks she's rich, just cos she's got her old-age pension.'

'Have you signed the forms for her, then, Raf?' asks Colette.

'Course he has,' says Kirsty. 'I saw it in the magazine.'

'That was a joke, dum dum,' says Raffy.

'Oh gosh,' says Colette. 'I missed it as well. Ha ha ha.'

'I bet Mrs Ainley didn't think it was a joke,' says Kirsty. 'Taking the piss out of her precious little forms.'

'Hard cheddar,' says Raffy. 'I told you. I won't be going, so what does it matter.'

Fred comes round, wiping down the white PVC tablecloths, emptying the overflowing ashtrays, clearing the tables, then clearing his throat. Letting his regular patrons know that he is getting ready to close for the evening.

'Where the hell are they?' says Kirsty.

'I'm having one more thing,' says Raffy, 'then I'm going. Beans on toast, perhaps. Anyone lend me the money?'

'And me. I'm starving,' says Colette. 'Can anybody lend me enough to buy a bar of chocolate?'

'Don't look at me,' says Kirsty. 'I'm broke.'

The door opens, and in burst Ella and Toby. They look very pleased with themselves. Raffy jumps up and immediately slaps them on the back, congratulating them on their success. He is in fact trying to remember where they have been and what they have been doing. Oh yeah, he thinks, that dopey Sixth-Form Committee meeting.

'So, is it teas all round, then?' says Raffy, smiling. 'To celebrate, huh?'

Ella looks at Toby, who nods and smiles. 'I'll get them,' he says, going to the counter.

'And a fancy,' pleads Colette, putting on her little-girl voice.

'Okay, then, just for you,' says Toby.

'So what happened?' asks Colette as Ella sits down.

'Hold on,' says Ella. 'We've run all the way from school.'

'All of two hundred metres,' says Kirsty. 'I'll tell your dad you're knackered after a titchy run.'

'I want to start at the beginning,' says Ella. 'Let's wait for Toby.'

'No, no,' says Raffy. 'Just give us the headlines, spare us the details. I've got to go soon. I've got a heavy date. Liz Ainley, she's called.'

'That's not funny,' says Kirsty.

'You haven't felt her,' says Raffy.

'Give it a rest, Raf,' says Colette.

'Well,' says Ella as Toby sits down, struggling with a tray of teas. 'We won, that's the main thing. Nobody voted against us. Just two abstained.'

'Who was that?' asks Colette.

'Mohammed and Halima.'

'Well, they would, wouldn't they,' says Raffy. 'Their old folks would go spare otherwise.'

'Yeah, well I know who will go spare now,' says Colette.

'Who?' asks Toby.

'Old Ma Potter,' says Colette.

'Ah, we've thought of that,' says Ella. 'Wait till you hear what we're going to do next.'

'Not more plots,' says Jules. 'You should both be in the Cabinet.'

The door opens and everyone turns round. It's Sam, out of breath, having run all of three hundred metres from home, worried that they might have left by now.

'Oh, I thought it was Dim,' says Colette, sitting down again.

'Disappointed?' asks Kirsty mischievously.

'Oh, desperately,' says Colette.

'So what's the answer?' asks Raffy as Sam joins them.

'Come on, Sam,' says Ella. 'Tell us quick.'

'You're on, Raffy,' says Sam. 'My mum's thrilled. In fact she's willing to take two. So if you'd like us to have your exchange girl, Colette, I'm sure we could put her up.'

'I'm sure you could, Sam,' says Raffy. 'You cheeky sod. Are you listening, Ella? He's trying to fix himself up with a bit of hot croissant, on tap.'

'Shurrup, Raffy,' says Sam, turning to face Colette. 'No really, Col, if it would help you out, my mum would be only too pleased. I know you're a bit cramped, and with your mum and that . . .'

'Do you mind,' says Colette, getting up. 'Nothing wrong with our flat. Or my mum.'

'Sorry,' says Sam, but Colette is putting on her coat, ready to go.

'Not waiting for Dim?' says Kirsty, again with a slight edge.

'Mind your own business,' says Colette, going out of the café and slamming the door.

'Oh, like that is it?' says Raffy. '*Quel dommage*. But not to worry. This is a happy evening. Time for celebrations, all round. For Ella and Toby, and for *moi*. Paris, here I come.

'I say, Fred, my good man. Cancel those beans on toast. Frogs' legs on toast, if you don't mind.'

'Too late,' grunts Fred. 'Everything's off. And I want you lot *out*.'

The phone rings, Fred's phone behind the counter, not to be used by customers.

'Sorry, we're closed,' says Fred into the receiver. 'What? This is a private phone. I don't take no messages . . . Urgent business? I dunno about that . . . Consultant of what? A board meeting, did you say? . . . Your what isn't working? . . . Fax? Fax for what? The memory? . . . Okay, I'll tell them. But just this once.'

Fred listens, nodding his head, then lumbers across to their table.

'Someone called Mr Dmitri. He's toured the establishment and likes what he sees. Now he's going for dinner with his business partners, so will you accept his excuses for not turning up this evening.'

Colette: cheered up

EPISODE 4

Asnières, Paris

Dear Colette,

Hello!! I am your new French fiend. I am seventeen and I am in the premier class at our lycée, here. Now, my hobbies are playing at table tennis, what you say pong-ping, computing (I have a Amstrad) listening some pop music, especially from Bruce Springsteen and U2. However, do you like Bros? Are they deaded? Where were they? From Liverpool? Nonetheless, I like watching television, especially all sports.

At the weekends I like go out with my friends and we make things. All the same, in the summer I often went camping with my Old Man and Old Woman! I am born in Marseilles, but I am living here since a long time, for example, six years. I am no brothers and sisters, just like you. But I am a grandfather. I'm looking forward to my visit with you and your parents. I never been to England before and I very curious of it. I have seen a lot of London in the television and it is very exciting I think with lots of fashions and different things to us. I like to stay with you a lot, in a typical home of Londoners, I think will be interesting. I have been to Germany with my school and she was very good. I think exchanges are very good for understandings, don't you?

Write me soon. Greetings to you and your parents.

Adeline

Breakfast time, Colette's home

Colette is sitting reading her post. There are two letters for her, probably a world record, plus lots of bills for her mother, still unopened. This is not exceptional.

'Oh God, Mum,' shouts Colette to her mother, who is still throwing things around in her bedroom as she gets ready for work. 'She likes Bruce Springsteen. What have I done?'

'Probably very little,' replies her mother. 'I bet you haven't written your letter yet.'

'You're sussed there,' says Colette. 'I wrote first, so bite on that.'

'Well, write again,' says her mother. 'Mrs Ainley said write as many letters beforehand as possible. You've got bags of time for once, so go on, do it now.'

'Stop hassling me, Mother.'

'But it's important you write straight back to her, so you can get to know each other.'

'Don't think I wanna know her. U2. Dear God! They're so out of touch, these Frogs.'

'And don't use that phrase. It's not respectful.'

'I bet they call us a lot worse things.'

'Two wrongs don't make a right.'

'Oh, belt up and get off to work.'

'How do I look, dear?' says Colette's mother, coming into their living room.

'Horrible,' says Colette, without looking up. 'As usual.'

'Can I read the letter?' asks her mother.

'No, it's personal,' says Colette, throwing it down on a chair. 'Anyway, I think I'll back out. It's not gonna work. We've just got no room in this lousy flat.'

'I've told you,' says her mother. 'I can sleep on the couch in here and she can have my bedroom. It's only five days. I can manage easily.'

'Don't be stupid. You'd turn this room into a dump, like you do everywhere. We wouldn't be able to use it, not if you were sleeping here with all your junk. Where would we watch telly, eat, do things? No, it wouldn't work. I'd better tell Mrs Ainley to count me out.'

'Right then, we'll just go back to the original plan. We'll put that spare mattress on your bedroom floor, and she can have the bed. That was a good idea of yours. There is room for two in there, if you're sensible. She obviously expects it. You said in your form she'd have to share, didn't you?'

'I dunno what I put. In my letter or the form.'

'Oh yes, you're very quick to scoff at other people's letters and their hobbies, but I bet your letter was no masterpiece of modern prose.'

'Look, you're giving me a headache. Get yourself off. You'll be late. And leave that bloody letter alone!'

'Language,' says Colette's mother, going into a corner and reading the letter. 'There you are, she's looking forward to it, coming to our typical London home. She knows exactly what the score is, so what are you worried about?'

'My rotten bedroom. It's titchy. And over-crowded.'

'Okay, you can put that pine chest of drawers in my room.'

'Thanks, Mum,' says Colette, smiling. This was what she was after. She has been campaigning for weeks to get rid of the chest of drawers. She would much prefer to keep all her clothes on an old metal coat-stand she has seen in Camden Lock market, but her mother has refused to let her buy it. She says she won't have such a stupid thing in the flat. And anyway, Colette would quickly go off it. Pine chests of drawers are always useful and cost a fortune now, so the answer so far has been no, definitely no.

'But it's only for the week,' says her mother. 'It's going back into your room afterwards. Don't get any ideas, miss.'

Colette smiles. The letter from Paris has in fact

cheered her up, made it all seem real. It's brought Adeline much nearer to her, even if she does appear to like crap music.

'It's a nice name, Adeline,' says her mother. 'I wonder if she gets called Adèle.'

'I wonder,' says Colette.

'It was what my grandmother called herself. Did you realize your great-grandmother was called Adeline? That's my father's mother, the one from Ireland.'

'How fascinating,' says Colette.

'It is, actually. There used to be this famous song in the olden days, "Sweet Adeline". Now, how does it go? Not sure if U2 have ever sung it, or Bruce Springtime. But they will, they will. Every good tune comes back.'

She starts to sing the song 'Sweet Adeline', till Colette shouts at her to stop.

'What's your other letter, dear?' asks her mother.

'I haven't opened it yet. I'm waiting till you go.'

'Actually,' says her mother, frowning hard, 'I think it's too warm for this dress. Perhaps I'll put on my multi-coloured –'

'Oh God, you're impossible,' shouts Colette as her mother goes back into the bedroom. She is smiling, though. 'You're just an old fish, so you are.'

Colette's flat, five minutes later

Colette's mother bounds into the living room. She is in a different outfit, but it is her suede suit, not the multi-coloured frock, despite the warm day. She stops when she sees Colette's face. Her smile has gone. She looks very near to tears.

'What's the matter?' asks her mother.

'Nothing, nothing.'

'Who's the other letter from?'

'Nobody. Just get off, will you?'

'I can't go now,' says her mother, 'leaving you all upset.'

'You'll be late,' says Colette blankly, the anger draining from her voice.

'I'm already late, so what does it matter. Come on, tell me.'

'It's Dim.'

'Dim? Writing a letter?'

'Yeah, that's the worst part. I know how hard it must have been for him, writing. I feel rotten. He's tried so hard.'

'To say what?'

'Oh, that I'm always on at him for not talking about his feelings. Just like all boys, really, but he takes it personally. He says he can't talk when he's with me cos I mock him if he ever starts. He says I keep putting him down, criticizing him. Then when we're with other people, I'm horrible to him, or just ignore him. Oh God, what a mess . . .'

'I feel sorry for him.'

'So do I,' says Colette. 'That's what tears me up. But I can't do anything about it. I like him as a friend, always have done, but he wants – I dunno, more. A commitment. He's even used that word. How phoney can you get?'

'That's not very fair,' says her mother.

'I know!' shouts Colette. 'I'm not being fair. I'm a bitch. It's all true, what he says.'

'No, it's not,' says her mother. 'I'm sure you're trying to be kind and spare his feelings. Perhaps you should have been tougher, made the position clear, even if it does hurt more at the time.'

'He says he hates ringing me. He has to force himself every time. He doesn't know what to say.'

'Boys don't –'

'Stop saying that!' shouts Colette. 'You don't know anything. He doesn't know what to say because he doesn't think. He just accepts. All the time I've known him I've had to organize everything – where we're going, getting the tickets, finding out the times, thinking of things. He does nothing. He's more concerned about his boring Maths problems or his stupid money-making schemes than thinking about me, going out with me.'

'Poor Dim.'

'Oh, shut up.'

'Perhaps going to Paris will help,' says her mother. 'You know, meeting different people. Getting away will give you a new perspective. You might be able to work out how you really feel about him, and about yourself.'

'Save the cheap psychology, Mother,' says Colette.

'Just trying to help.'

'The thing is,' says Colette, 'he's so sweet, really. And kind. Like a big soppy dog.'

'Ahh,' says her mother.

'But he's just working himself up, really.'

41

'How do you mean?'

'Just deciding to get himself in this position. We've been sort of going out for two terms now, off and on. Just good friends, all that. But the moment I try to tell him that that's all it is, I don't want to be committed, he suddenly gets all this nonsense into his head.'

'And have you been trying to tell him?'

'Yeah, in a sort of way.'

'Well, perhaps you should write it all down as well. Make it clear to him, so he knows.'

'Oh God, all you want me to do is write letters. You're worse than a bloody teacher.'

Colette picks up Dim's letter, scrunches it up in her hands and throws it on the floor. Her mother moves towards it.

'Don't!' shouts Colette. 'Just you dare.'

She looks around the table, then grabs a packet of cornflakes. She throws it, as hard as possible, in the direction of her mother, but the packet is almost empty and doesn't reach her.

'Oh God, I'm so furious,' shouts Colette. 'I just want to scream and scream . . .'

'Hold on,' says her mother. 'I might be able to help.'

She goes to a cupboard and pulls out a box of old plates, cups and saucers, all neatly packed. 'These were going to the school jumble, but I can think of a better use for them.'

She lays down sheets of newspaper on the kitchen's wooden floor, then empties out the box of crockery.

'There you go. Smash them all, my dear. Break them with your hands, jump on them, throw them on the ground. It's up to you.'

Colette looks at her mother in amazement. Her friends often think she is eccentric and does strange things, though Colette herself rarely finds anything unusual about her mother. Unless she's being unusually annoying or amusing. But this is the first time her mother has encouraged her to commit actual vandalism.

'Come on,' says her mother. 'I want to watch this.'

'I think you're potty,' says Colette.

'It's all rubbish. It will save me taking the box to school. Smash 'em all up, then I'll put them straight in the bin as I go out.'

Colette bends down and picks up a Royal Wedding commemorative mug. She looks at it carefully. It's stained and chipped, but she remembers it well. She can recall the day she was given it at junior school, when Lady Di and Prince Charles got married. She holds it high, staring at it, then opens her fingers and lets it fall. There is a most satisfying cracking, splintering noise.

Next, she smashes two bowls together, both Mr Men bowls, neither of which she ever liked. She hurls a Beatrix Potter plate on the floor, stamps on a Woolworth's cup and saucer in horrible purple, then breaks to smithereens a nasty ashtray, stolen from a pub. Very soon, every item is in fragments.

'There', says her mother, sweeping the debris into a pile and putting it all back into the cardboard box, which she then ties with string. 'Feel better, huh?'

'Yeah, thanks,' says Colette, smiling.

'Let's go, then,' says her mother, picking up her attaché case along with the cardboard box.

'God, you'll be so late,' says Colette.

'It doesn't matter,' says her mother.

'Tell you what,' says Colette. 'I'll write you a note, just for a change. "Dear Boss, please excuse my mum, only she has been busy this morning on a therapy session with a deprived, silly, mixed-up teenager. Yours and oblige, Colette."'

She gives her mother a hug, and they go out together.

Raffy: *le handsome et sensational*

EPISODE 5

Mon cher amis,
Bonjour, comment ça va et tout cela stuff. Toujours la politess, I always dit. Ici votre ami de Londres qui est writing à vous lot, comme la old bat nous command. Je veux à put you tout dans la picture, ecole wise. Okay, allons, mes petites choux.

Premierly, notre ecole est appelling itself St Andrews Road School. C'est parce que de la rue dans lequel le school is, si vous attrapez mon drift. Les enfants, 'scuse moi, les etudiants, comme nous dans le Sixth aimons à penser we are, we appelons ourselves les S.T.A.R.S. Gerrit? C'est un acronym. Regard votre dictionaire, dum dum, must be là. Je sais le mot pour star. Etoile, nesspa? Bon, huh. Je ne suis pas thick, oh non. J'ai B dans le GCSE à prover it.

Nous habitons le nord du Londres. C'est le plus best part du monde. Si vous habitez le sud de Londres, sous le river, vous etes dans dead shtook. C'est un place de merde. Ne personne, but ne personne, habits dans le sud, sauf les scrubbers et les thickos. Dans le sud, comme dans le nord de Angleterre, en fact any place nord du Watford, ils sont tous la same. Ils mangent leur babies. Je kid vous non.

Notre ecole, sur le whole, generalement speaking, tous choses considered, est crap. Il y a des exceptions, mais pour le moment je ne peux pas penser de any. Le best est le Sixieme, ainsi vous lot etes heureux blighters parce que vous avez missed le rubbish. Mais nous avons un brill chambre de common, and certain brillos etudiants, lequel je viens to dans un moment.

Il y a huit personnes venant à your place et je will explique some of them, bientot, sorry maintenant. Etes vous ready? Pay attention.

La sexiest de les gels est la belle Taz. Ne touche pas, cos je will battre vous lot, sharpish. Elle est formidable. Je serrai tres angry si je catch vous sods attemptant le hanky panky avec elle. Taz est une mystere, pas de question. Her pere has beaucoup de dosh, mais ne pas dite anyone que je said so.

Alors, il y a la belle Colette, equalement sexy mais ne pas si mysterious. Le mauvais news est elle a un grand boyfriend, tres grand, avec grand muscles, qui ne dite pas beaucoups. Le bon news est il ne vient pas à Paris, cos il est un thicko scientist, ainsi any de vous jokers can peut etre attempter votre main avec Colette. Et bon chance, vive la difference, connais que je mean.

Jules est aussi going à Paris. Il est un garcon, je pense. Il wears les pantalons et il vais au bogs with les garcons. Il pense que il est le best dressed dude dans le mond entire. Quel joke, 'scuse moi quand je laugh, ha ha ha. Il spend un fortune sur son stuff. Regard le gel sur son bonce. Quel pouf, si vous demande à moi. Tout la meme, Jules est un bon laugh, si vous aimez un bon laugh.

Finalement, il y a le merveilleux, le handsome, le sensational, l'un et seulement, Raffy. Probablement vous avez heard de him, nesspa? Il est le plus intelligent et le plus sexy garcon dans la ecole, dans Londres, dans l'universe.

Naturellement, il y a beaucoups de filles qui will desire le above-mentioned garcon, ainsi je suggest que vous send moi vos photographies, toot de sweet, nu si possible. Tous offers serra consideré dans total confidence. Apres ça, je serrai write back à vous and dire lesquels birds le bold Raffy would aime, et dans le quel order. Le motto de Raffy is à votre service. Dites ne plus.

Neanmoins – c'est un vraiment stupid mot Français, et mon dew, vous avez un lot of them. Et maintenant. Ainsi. Alors. Etcetera. Il faut que je finish cet lettre comme maintenant je vais sur le job, nudge nudge. Non, juste un petit joke. J'ai de homework to do. Autrement (c'est un nicer mot, je pense) la old bat serra moaning à moi demain. Elle appele herself Mme Ainley et elle est coming à Paris aussi, avec nous. Attendez until vous get un butcher's. Elle est une scream. Elle wears la mini. Quel legs! Quel knickers! Flut, zut, scut alors. Vous avez been warned.

Tout la best, regard vous soon. Les cheers, from tous dans la Sixth Français de S.T.A.R.S. de Londres du Nord . . .

Saturday, lunchtime, school
sports area

Raffy and Jules are in a lather, rushing around shifting tables and benches, working terribly hard.

'I'm knackered,' says Raffy. 'Okay for you. I've already done a morning's work.'

'What do you mean?' says Jules. 'I'm missing the highlight of my week, just for this. I'm usually in South Molton Street on a Saturday afternoon, or up the King's Road.'

'God, they'll all go bankrupt without your custom.'

'And my hands,' says Jules. 'Look at my hands! I wasn't meant for this nasty menial work.'

They both take a breather, only to be screamed at by one of the parents: Spike, a mainstay of the PTA. He has organized most school functions since records began, or as long as any other parent can remember.

'What are you two doing?' shouts Spike. 'Stop skiving at once and get over there. There's more cars to come in yet.'

It's the afternoon of the school's car boot sale and

Jules and Raffy are two of the helpers. For five years, neither of them has helped with a school jumble sale, fair, auction or any other sort of event. Jules considers such activities decidedly naff, not to say vulgar. Raffy considers any unpaid work a stupid waste of time.

'Look at all the rubbish they're hoping to sell,' says Jules as they walk down the lines of cars which have already parked, watching people unloading and setting out their wares. 'Pathetic. Absolutely pathetic.'

'Oh, I dunno,' says Raffy. 'One person's rubbish is another person's treasure. I don't call it pathetic. They don't feel the pathos themselves.'

'So what's your definition of pathetic?' asks Jules.

'I think you must be aware of your own pathos to be really pathetic.'

'Such as?'

'Well, let's say, watching *Top of the Pops* on your own,' says Raffy. 'The only slight pleasure in watching it at all is when you're with other people, so you can rubbish it together. So, if you are watching on your own, then a) you know you've got no friends and b) you must be hard up, to have nothing better to do. To me, that's true pathos.'

'Got you!' screams Spike, jumping out from behind an old Ford Escort. He has followed them down the next row of cars, suspecting they were going to disappear. 'What a couple of plonkers. Cut the philosophy and get over to those cars, like I told you.'

'Sorry, Spike,' says Raffy.

'Sorry, sir,' says Jules.

'I dunno,' says Spike. 'Every year, the volunteers get more and more useless.'

'Volunteers?' groans Raffy.

'Huh,' sighs Jules.

Meanwhile, at the front gates of the school

Colette and Taz are straining to keep back what appears to be a very angry football crowd. They are being pushed and pummelled, then verbally harangued by a bossy parent called Pippa, another PTA stalwart.

'Don't let anyone in till I tell you!' commands Pippa.

'But I just can't control them,' says Taz.

'*Courage, mes braves,*' hisses Pippa.

'Oh Gawd,' says Colette. 'That's just what we need. All this and bloody GCSE French.'

'*Right! Open the gates!*'

Pippa yells the order, adoring her moment of power. Colette and Taz are almost knocked flat by the avalanche, but manage to keep on their feet, struggling to take 20p from every punter. Children, the unwaged and pensioners are, of course, free.

'Don't let anyone sneak in,' yells Pippa.

She has taken up a position at one side of the drive, leaving Colette and Taz to guard the other side.

'I never realized money was so filthy,' says Taz. 'Just look at my hands, already.'

'Poor you,' says Colette. 'I did mean to tell you what money looks like. I suppose you've always thought it was rectangular and made of plastic, with your father's name on it.'

'Ha ha,' says Taz.

'Hello, girls,' says a man's voice. It's Mr Graham, Sam's father, giving them a wink. He has arrived late, rather breathless. He never misses a school sale, hoping to get bargains for his own Camden Lock market stall, but usually he manages to be among the first to get in.

'Women,' corrects Colette.

'More like drudges,' says Taz, mopping her brow.

'Anyway, how's it going, women?'

'Well, the rush is over now, I suppose,' says Colette, sitting down on a wooden box.

'Stand up, girl!' shouts Pippa.

'See you later,' says Mr Graham, smiling and walking in.

'Yeah, see you,' says Colette.

'He didn't pay!' yells Pippa. 'That man. You just let him through!'

'Oh, did I?' says Colette. 'Sorry about that.'

'I really don't know what's happening these days,' says Pippa. 'The standard of student volunteers is utterly abysmal.'

Later, at the sports area

The afternoon has gone very well, thanks to the good weather, which is always vital for a car boot sale. Spike and Pippa are busy counting up all the takings, but Spike is still keeping an eye on Raffy and Jules in case they slope off. Taz and Colette have been allowed to go, but they will be needed back again soon, to help clear up the debris. If the place is a mess, Mr Fish the caretaker will complain, and make problems for the next PTA event.

'A pity it couldn't have been next week,' says Jules. 'We could have brought all the French lot here.'

'Don't talk about it,' says Raffy. 'I'm worried about what we're going to do with them. What if they turn out to be a load of wallies?'

Toby and Ella appear, both carrying bundles of the sixth-form magazine, though neither has many left. It was Toby's idea to coincide publication of the latest issue with the car boot sale, to catch the crowds.

'Have you got your copy, sir?' Ella asks Spike.

'Yes, bought one earlier,' says Spike. 'Load of rubbish.'

'Especially the French stuff,' says Pippa. 'I don't know what they teach you at this school these days. Never seen such terrible French grammar in all my life.'

'Anyway,' says Spike, 'thanks for volunteering. We've taken more money today than ever before.'

'You volunteered?' says Ella to Raffy and Jules, incredulous.

'Yeah, didn't you hear?' says Raffy. 'Jolly good of us.'

'Actually, Liz Ainley volunteered for us,' says Jules. 'She managed to persuade the PTA that some profits from the sale would go towards the

French exchange. So we all had to volunteer, as we'll all benefit.'

'Especially me,' says Raffy. 'I'm definitely going now. For free.'

'Lucky Paris,' says Jules.

Jules: oh, so smarmy

EPISODE 6

Outside Victoria railway
station, Monday

The traffic wardens are on patrol, ready to shoot
from the hip, then pow, demolish every wallet with
one blow of their ticket books. Tough-looking
policemen, one or two of whom appear well over
thirteen, and several with real moustaches, are also
on duty. They are tramping up and down in pairs,
looking out for criminals, such as runaway kids from
the provinces, or really serious offenders, like
drivers parked on double yellow lines.

Inside a nondescript, beaten-up minibus sit nine
rather tense, worried people. A large middle-aged
woman in a short skirt is at the wheel, while eight
others sit with their faces pressed against the side
windows.

54

'We've been seen,' says the driver, in a heavy Lancashire accent. 'Oh God, now we're for it. Here they come.'

Are they planning a pay-roll job? Could they be drug runners? Or are they about to abduct some innocent French teenagers, lost in the Big Smoke? The latter would be a good guess, perhaps C plus for trying, or even a B for imagination.

'Let's pretend we're foreign,' says Raffy. 'No speeka da Eenglish. They might take pity on us.'

'Like hell,' says Mrs Ainley. 'They're buggers round here.'

'Language, language,' says Colette.

'I don't want to be fined,' says Mrs Ainley. 'Or clamped.'

'Well, let's go round the block again,' suggests Taz. 'We're still ten minutes early.'

'It'll take forever, with all the one-way systems,' says Mrs Ainley. 'And there's something on at Buckingham Palace. That's what's making the traffic really hellish.'

'Tell you what,' says Jules, sliding open the back door, 'I'll get out with Colette. We'll check the arrival platform, see if the train's on time, meet them, then pick you up back here.'

They jump out just as the wardens arrive, note-books at the ready, along with the fuzz, looking for trouble.

'Awfully sorry, officers,' smarms Jules. 'Hospital emergency service. But we're off now.'

'Oh yeah,' says a policeman.

Jules closes the rear door, revealing the

S.T.A.R.S. logo which denotes St Andrews Road School, and the minibus moves off.

'Truly,' says Jules. 'That just happens to be a Variety Club of Great Britain, sponsored minibus.'

Inside Victoria station

Colette is quite pleased to be in the advance welcome party. She's put on her best navy-blue striped T-shirt. It was a slight shock horror to see Taz wearing a similar one, though with narrower stripes and a lot more expensive. Taz has also got sun specs with her, what a bore, but no one else has thought of wearing a beret. Just a little joke. But Colette's own.

She and Jules push their way through the crowds, most of whom are standing as if in a trance. Colette has to take her specs off to examine the Arrivals board.

'What a drag,' she says to Jules. 'Half an hour late.'

'I'm afraid the boat train usually is,' says Jules.

'What we gonna do?' says Colette.

'You mean for the next half hour, or the next five days?'

'Both.'

'It's the five days that worry me,' says Jules. 'How are we going to entertain them? It's such a responsibility.'

'Okay for you,' says Colette. 'You've got a big flat. I'm going to be sleeping with my exchange, jammed right beside her in my titchy bedroom. What if I hate her? There will be no escape.'

'Let's go and see if the minibus has come back yet.'

They go outside and check the meeting place, but there's no sign of Mrs Ainley and the others. They stand on the pavement, waiting, wondering what the eight French kids will be like. Will it all be a mistake, or will this exchange lead to some new and wonderful relationships?

Taxis and minicabs draw up and let out their passengers. Most of the minicabs look very dodgy, the drivers as well as their cars. They wave their hairy arms and ring-covered fingers at any young person who is standing alone looking lost and hopeless, offering to give them a lift. There are a great many of these young people, resigned and exhausted, their innocent faces looking pinched and deprived. They stand by their belongings, moving on when drivers try to hassle them, or too many single men try to chat them up. They push their mobile bags, their mobile lives, a few yards along the pavement, pretending to the world that they are neither homeless, nor runaways, nor have they been stood up.

'Some of them are so sad and pathetic,' says Colette. 'Imagine arriving in London, all on your own. It must be hellish.'

'Imagine arriving in Paris,' says Jules.

That makes Colette pause and think for a moment, thankful that she is going on her first proper trip abroad with a party. A day trip to Boulogne with her mother, some years ago, doesn't count.

'Look at her,' says Jules, nodding towards the

57

scruffiest, most deprived-looking girl of all. 'Just asking for it. Jail-bait, that's what I'd say.'

'Shall we ask her if she wants help?' says Colette. 'Offer her money for a phone, perhaps?'

A gleaming Range Rover draws up with a screech of brakes. The deprived-looking waif bounds forward, tears open the door and in accents of pure Sloane, screams at the driver.

'Where the — have you been? And why the — was Mummy not here when she promised?'

Colette and Jules smile at each other. 'Yup, it's always dangerous to categorize people,' says Jules.

There is still no sign of the minibus, so they check watches. They realize it's only two minutes till the boat train arrives, so they turn and rush back into the station, heading for the right platform.

'How will we know them without Liz?' says Colette.

'Don't think she would help much anyway,' says Jules. 'It's a new teacher, apparently, in charge of them. A bloke. Someone she hasn't met.'

'Right, we'll just have to stop any group that looks French.'

'You mean wearing berets and smelling of garlic,' says Jules. 'Hey, you're not half French are you, Col?'

The whole train appears to be full of French people, mostly school children on their spring trips, jabbering away and shouting at each other while distraught teachers rush around, convinced someone has already got lost.

'I think that's them,' says Jules. 'Look, there's a

small group coming down the platform. They look about our age. You ask.'

'No, you ask,' says Colette. 'Your French is better. I don't even know how to pronounce that place they come from. Asnières, or whatever it is.'

Jules clears his throat, tries out several versions, then marches up to the party, approaching them with his best smile. He introduces himself and asks if they are from Asnières. They are indeed. And their teacher speaks perfect English, so Jules is able to save his French for another time.

They all walk down the platform together. The French students look embarrassed yet aloof, shy yet cool, not saying anything, pretending to look around at the other passengers, at the station architecture and the passing bookstalls, but secretly eyeing up Jules and Colette, their new English friends, taking in every item of clothing, as these two walk ahead with their teacher.

Jules drops back a bit, smiling and saying hi, trying to be welcoming. He doesn't get very far. Colette is still walking with the French teacher, asking him his name and if he's been to London before.

She suddenly appears to become convulsed, stopping and choking, so Jules rushes forward and begins to slap her back. This little incident lightens the atmosphere, as all the French students also stop and make sympathetic noises around Colette, until eventually she recovers.

The school's minibus is waiting outside, engine revving. Raffy and two other boys jump out of the back and quickly load in all the baggage belonging to the French party, while Mrs Ainley pulls open the sliding doors at the side and ushers them all in. They just manage to drive away before the traffic wardens arrive.

'Oh God, you won't believe it,' says Colette, whispering in Raffy's ear. She starts on another convulsion, and has to be thumped on the back till her laughter subsides.

'Wait till Ella and Toby hear,' says Colette, laughing again.

'Look, stop messing around,' says Raffy. 'You're dribbling in my ear.'

'Guess what,' says Colette. 'Their master is called Condom. Monsieur Condom. In this week of all weeks.'

'Perfect timing,' says Raffy. 'I look forward to seeing his name on the petition.'

Inside the minibus, St Andrews Road, half an hour later

Mrs Ainley is very kindly taking everyone home, each sixth former with his or her respective exchange. Half have already been dropped off, along with their baggage.

Taz, Colette, Jules and Raffy are sitting at the back of the bus together, still not quite sure who is going with whom. They were all introduced at the station, the French students shaking hands with their new English friends, but neither side could take in all the different names.

Mrs Ainley stops outside Sam's house, near the

school, to let Raffy off with his partner, who is called Didier. He is going to sleep at Sam's for the next five nights, but Raffy will come and see him every day. Didier is tall and thin, wears spectacles and looks rather serious. Raffy makes faces behind his back as they get off.

'You won't forget, then?' Raffy shouts to Colette, Jules and Taz. 'See you at the pub at eight. Don't be late.'

The French all look very excited, turning and beaming at Taz, Colette and Jules.

'Zat is what I most want to do in London,' says one of them, an attractive girl called Blanche. The others giggle.

Blanche is Taz's partner and they are the next to get off. Blanche is very lively, with a husky voice, always chattering and giggling. Raffy has already lined her up as potential chat-up material, which is why he's so keen for them all to meet in the pub.

Jules, who lives not too far away from Taz, is dropped off next, with his partner, Pierre. Pierre is dark-haired, short and sensitive-looking. He's probably got hidden passions, or so Colette thinks. She has been carefully studying the back of his neck on the way from the station.

It is only when Pierre gets off that Colette realizes something has gone wrong. Where is her exchange girl, Adeline? Colette looked out for Adeline earlier, trying hard to catch her name amid all the introductions at Victoria, but presumed she had missed hearing it. The only people remaining on the bus now, apart from Mrs Ainley, are Monsieur

Condom and another person she presumes is also a teacher. Quite a nice-looking man, whom both she and Taz had compared notes on at Victoria. He is young, wearing a suit and sun specs, and has a small moustache and a neat beard.

'This is your house, isn't it, Colette?' says Mrs Ainley, checking a list in front of her, putting away her *A-Z*.

'Yes, miss,' says Colette. 'But my girl isn't here.'

'What?'

'She's called Adeline,' says Colette. 'And she hasn't turned up.'

'I am Adeline,' says the young man with the beard. 'Jean-Louis Adeline. How do you do?'

'Oh, *enchanté*,' says Colette, astonished rather than enchanted.

Mrs Ainley helps Jean-Louis out quickly with his bags. He is the last and she wants to get off home with Monsieur Condom, who is staying at her house. 'There must have been a mix-up, Colette,' she says. 'But you'll cope, I'm sure. Let me know if your mother objects.'

'You are Colette?' asks Jean-Louis, smiling, as they stand on the pavement together.

'Yes, I am,' says Colette, looking for her keys.

'But you have a French name. How come is that?'

'Just my mum, I suppose. How come *you* have a girl's name?'

'Jean-Louis, it is a boy's name.'

'I know, but you signed yourself Adeline?'

'That is the English style, is it not? The English are so correct. I read in an English school story how it is that all the teachers they call pupils by their second name. Is this not true?'

'Not any more,' says Colette. 'That was yonks ago.'

'What is this "yonks"?'

'Oh, I'll tell you later,' says Colette, leading the way up the stairs to her flat, fingers crossed that her mother will be in and can quickly and quietly sort out the accommodation problem before Jean-Louis sees that Colette's mattress has been set up right alongside his bed.

What will he think of English girls if he sees that?

The Cow and Bull, much later that night

After some initial shyness, with the French students sitting together and talking in French while the English talked together in English, they have all become friends. It was Jules's idea to split everyone up and sit alternately, French and English. That was what made each of them try a bit harder.

'So, what do you want to do this week, then?' asks Raffy.

'We are looking forward to experiencing the English education system,' says Didier.

'Oh, my good Gawd,' says Colette, in her best cockney accent. Immediately Blanche imitates her, getting the intonation right straight away. After that, Blanche insists on saying this phrase all the time.

'Forget all that cobblers,' says Raffy. 'I mean that rubbish.'

'What is "rubb-eesh"?' asks Blanche.

'Everything you don't like. You just say it's rubbish.'

'So you are rubb-eesh, yes?' she says to Raffy, beaming.

'Exactly,' says Colette. 'You got it right away.'

'Surely what you really want in London,' says Raffy, smiling at Blanche, pleased that she is bothering to tease him, 'is a good time, not any boring school work. That's what I want in Paris – a good time. Wuhay the lads. Here we go, here we go, here we go . . .'

'Here we go where?' asks Didier. 'Here we go round the mulberry bush? We have learned that at school. Shall I sing it to you, yes?'

'No, save it for closing time,' says Raffy. 'Give everyone a treat.'

'I want to go to Heaven,' says Blanche.

'You've come to the right place, darling,' says Raffy. 'I know the way to get girls straight to heaven.'

'She means the club, dum dum,' says Jules.

'What is "dum dum"?' asks Blanche.

Raffy explains, and Blanche adds another phrase to her repertoire.

'It used to be a gay club,' says Jules. 'I'm not even sure if it's still open.'

'I want to go to Carnaby Street,' says Pierre.

'Darling,' says Jules, 'you certainly do not. No one staying in my place goes anywhere near Carnaby Street. I'll take you to the really good places.'

'I want to go to Tottingham Hotspur,' says Jean-Louis.

'Oh, my good Gawd,' says Raffy. 'I thought you followed football.'

'I do. I like Tottingham Hotspur.'

'That proves you don't,' says Raffy.

'It's his little joke,' says Colette. 'He's an Arsenal supporter. Just ignore him.'

'So Tottingham is rubb-eesh, you dum dum, oh, my good Gawd,' says Blanche, and everyone laughs.

More drinks are ordered. Jules, Taz, Colette and Raffy are drinking glasses of wine in honour of their new friends, much to the horror of the four French. None of them, so they say, ever drinks wine when they go out. It's either coke or beer. Tonight they are trying a little beer.

'By the end of the week, Blanche,' says Raffy, 'we'll teach you some really useful words. All quite short. Four-letter words, in fact, which you can try out on Monsieur Condom.'

At the very mention of his name, they all laugh again, then explain to the French students what the joke is.

'But it's quite a usual French name,' says Didier. 'We have a famous French rugby player called Condom. He is very good on the ball.'

This has the English contingent all laughing once again.

'In London,' says Blanche, 'what I really want to do is get drunk.'

'Oh, my good Gawd,' says Jean-Louis. Colette smiles. So he has got a sense of humour after all, she thinks. Perhaps it won't be so bad, him staying at her place.

Near Colette's flat

Colette and Jean-Louis are walking home, chatting away, both rather merry. They all stayed at the pub till closing-time. Colette is thinking how useful it is having a boy living with her, when it comes to going home at night. Taz and Blanche have got the benefit of Jules and Pierre to see them home, but Colette lives in completely the opposite direction from the others. Getting home is always a problem for her. Unless she is with Dim. And she is still trying not to be with Dim.

'Taz, she is very nice,' says Jean-Louis.

'She is. She's lovely. Best-dressed person in the Sixth. And very nice.'

'She has boyfriend?' asks Jean-Louis.

'Not really,' says Colette, thinking hard, deciding to give the impression that perhaps Taz does have a boyfriend. 'Well, sort of.'

'Oh,' says Jean-Louis, rather disappointed.

'You have a girlfriend in Paris?'

'Sort of,' says Jean-Louis.

They arrive at Colette's home. She tells him to follow her up the stairs as quietly as possible, then she carefully opens the door of their flat. Her mother is still not back, which is strange, though she did say there was a farewell party on in her office and she might be late.

Colette offers to make Jean-Louis coffee, but he says he is too tired. It has been a long day.

'I want you to take me straight to bed, please,' says Jean-Louis. Colette swallows deeply, cursing her mother.

She shows Jean-Louis into her mother's room, where she has already placed his case. She told him earlier he would be sleeping there, but she had hoped her mother would be back by now to clear out the mess. She says goodnight to Jean-Louis, closes his door, then quickly writes a note for her mother. It explains what has happened and tells her mother she will be on the sofabed in the living room, the plan which she herself suggested.

Colette falls asleep quickly, dreaming about Jean-Louis's little beard, taking it off and discovering that it's not real but stuck on with glue. She is awakened just after midnight by loud screams from her mother's bedroom. Then she hears her mother staggering out, shouting her name, obviously rather the worse for wear. She has come back from the party, stumbled in, and not read the note. And got into bed, beside Jean-Louis.

'Oh, my good God,' Jean-Louis is saying, over and over again.

Toby: travelling salesman

EPISODE 7

KNOW YOUR ENGLISH!
(Or: 'No, you're English?')

Bienvenue, my cuddly cabbages, my little sticks of *lycée* liquorice, my friendly Froggies. *Sixth Censored* is going to help you improve your English word power. Before setting off to explore the capital, it will pay to test your knowledge.

Get your crayons and *plumes* out, my little sprouts.

1. British pupils are known for their politeness. When asked to do something by a teacher, which is the correct reply?
   a) 'On your bike.'
   b) 'Get lost, fatface.'
   c) 'Piss off, you old baggage.'

68

2. On entering a sixth-form common room, it is customary to:
   a) Say excuse me
   b) Take one's hat off
   c) Belch

3. The Princess of Wales is:
   a) Married to Prince Harry
   b) A fashion model
   c) A railway locomotive

4. Queen Elizabeth is:
   a) A corgi
   b) A ship
   c) A pub

5. Oxford Street is:
   a) On the way to Oxford
   b) On the way from Oxford
   c) London's most famous street for shoplifters

6. Who lives at 10, Downing Street?
   a) The Queen
   b) A policeman
   c) Nobody, the Government is selling it

7. What is the connection between the following? Cliff Richard; George Michael; Mrs Potter; Jack the Ripper

8. Correct the following Charles Dickens titles: *The Tale of Two Kitties*; *Oliver Twist and Shout*; *David Copperbottom*; *Hard Cheddar*; *Good Vibrations*

9. Which of these plays did Shakespeare write?
   All's Well That's Arsenal; McDonald's; A Midsummer Wet Dream; As You Asked; The Temptress; The Merry Wives of Henry VIII; Much Ado about Bugger All; Two Gentlemen of Valderma

10. True or false?
    In winter, the London streets are full of figs; If you want to know the time, ask a London bus; All pillar boxes wear bowler hats; They only change the guards when their underpants are dirty; An Englishman's home is his shop; Scotsmen keep thistles under their kilts; Welshmen repair leaks; Genius comes from Ireland

Answers: *Questions 1–6:* If you got mostly a)s, better stay at home, Frogling; mostly b)s, resit one year; all c)s, welcome to St Andrews' sixth form.
Question 7: None of them has been caught and punished for their crimes.
Question 8: Don't be stupid. They were all sung on last week's *Top of the Pops*.
Question 9: Trick question. Jeffrey Archer wrote them all.
Question 10: They're rubbish, just like you, dum dum.

School, sixth-form common room, Friday lunchtime

'Where are they all?' asks Toby, walking round trying to sell copies of the latest issue of the sixth-form magazine.

'Who?' asks Colette.

'The French,' says Toby. 'We've got a piece here which I'm sure they'll love.'

'Oh, them,' says Colette. 'I dunno.'

'They all came in the first morning, dead early,' says Raffy. 'Then the second morning, half of them came late. Now it's their last day, none of them have turned up at all, except for Didier. He's a right creep. I'm not dragging him out of the library again.'

'They're probably all still in bed,' says Colette.

'Yeah – with whom?' says Raffy. 'Can't all be sleeping with your mum.'

'That's not funny,' says Colette. 'It only happened the first night, you know that. We've hardly seen Jean-Louis. Not since he met Kirsty.'

Raffy is about to make a few nasty comments, but restrains himself. He knows that for him, too, like Colette, things have not quite worked out the way he expected. Blanche has decided that the only hunky, chunky, groovy feller in the whole sixth form worth going out with is – Dim. Much to Raffy's fury.

Raffy puts her infatuation down to the generous hospitality which somehow Dim is managing to lavish on her. It can't be because of any natural charm or quick wit, as, of course, Raffy has the

71

monopoly on those. He's holding out higher hopes of Paris, when Dim won't be there. Colette is looking forward to having less competition in France as well. Kirsty will be at home and Taz is not really a rival, as people soon give up chasing the unattainable.

'What are we going to do with them tonight?' Jules asks Colette and Raffy. 'All of them are expecting something really good for their last night. I think they're a bit fed-up with Fred's, and even the Cow and Bull. They keep going on about the famous London clubs.'

'They cost a bomb,' says Colette.

'And we'll never get sixteen tickets anyway.'

'Yeah, Taz has tried the Town and Country,' says Jules. 'All sold out for tonight. Friday's their big evening.'

'Bring them to our campaign meeting,' says Toby. 'That should be jolly interesting for them.'

'Rapture,' says Raffy. 'They'll love that.'

'What stage is it at now, then?' says Jules. 'I haven't followed it this week, with the French lot being here.'

'Don't you read the magazine properly? Here, on page three: CONDOM CAMPAIGN: THE FINAL THRUST.'

'Good headline,' says Raffy.

'Yeah, Kirsty thought of it.'

'Remind me,' says Jules. 'Where's it at, exactly?'

'Well,' says Toby. 'You know we got a motion passed by the Sixth-Form Committee, unanimously, to have condom machines in both lavatories.'

'About time,' says Raffy. 'What's wrong with having them in every classroom? All for free, I hope.'

'If you're going to be silly . . .' says Toby.

'Sorry, sir,' says Raffy. 'No, it is a good idea, and I hope you haven't forgotten who thought it up. I'm just sorry I've been so frightfully busy, tied up with these Frogs. Or not tied up, as it happens.'

'We decided not to go officially to Mrs Potter for the next stage,' continues Toby. 'Not yet. We know she'd just turn it down flat.'

'Good thinking,' says Raffy. 'You could be right there.'

'Instead, we're going straight to the governors. We've looked up the rules and regulations, and the Board of Governors are technically in charge of the school. They hire the staff. They agree to everything. They are legally in control.

'So, we've lobbied the five parent governors, and all are on our side.'

'Hey, that's amazing.'

'Took a lot of doing, but Ella was brilliant. They all saw we mean it seriously, not as a joke. We're all over sixteen, and condoms are right in line with official Government policy.'

'Right on, brother,' says Raffy.

'The resolution's on the agenda for the governors' meeting on Monday evening. That will be the big one, the meeting which will decide what happens.'

'Oh, what a shame,' says Raffy. 'We'll be in Paris. It's our first night. What do you think, Col? Should we cancel and not go? How can we possibly miss such excitement?'

Friday evening, somewhere in darkest Kentish Town

They are all together in a pub, or at least trying to be all together in a pub. The first problem is that there are eight of them: Colette, Raffy, Jules, Taz and Kirsty, plus three French students, Didier, Pierre and Jean-Louis. The second problem is that the pub is already chocka, standing room only, and even then you have to be lucky to be able to stand. Thirdly, it's practically pitch black, one of those artily-craftily lit pubs where the decor is dark and the lighting almost non-existent.

'Oh, let's go home,' says Taz. 'You can all come back to my place and have something to eat. My father has invited all of you.'

Taz didn't want to come out at all, especially not to Kentish Town or to this sort of pub, but she feels she had to, it being the French students' last night. She promised Blanche she would. She's her sup- posed exchange, though she has hardly seen Blanche all week. And now, this evening, of all evenings, Blanche has disappeared.

'Thank you, but no,' says Pierre. 'I like your English pubs. This has been the best one we have had experience of.'

Taz looks around. There is a strobe light going off and on, freezing people into white fluorescent stripes one minute, then blue the next. Customers at the bar are watching the door, looking out for newcomers, then glaring at them. They all look like they want a fight, pushing and shoving each other, yelling and shouting.

Jules doesn't like it either. He feels threatened. Most people are young, late teens or early twenties. They seem so ugly and badly dressed to Jules, long-haired, in drab clothes. Leftover hippies, bearded and scruffy, with staring eyes and leering mouths.

'Let's go to the Cow and Bull,' says Jules. 'Even that is better than this place.'

'I don't know why you dragged us here, Raffy,' says Colette.

'Hold on,' says Raffy. 'I told you. It's got great music. You all said you wanted live music.'

'We've changed our minds,' says Jules. 'Let's go. I'd rather have muzak.'

The French students are staring around, mesmerized, taking it all in. Several people are staring back at them, hoping for some aggro. Colette is worried that one of their group will either get picked upon or go missing in the crush, and they'll spend the rest of the evening searching for him or her.

'It's at the back, the music,' says Raffy. 'Can't you hear it, Jules?'

'Bloody awful,' says Jules.

'But you can't say it's not live,' says Raffy. 'You lot hold on here, I'll fight my way through and see if we can get in.'

'I come with you?' offers Jean-Louis. He could be a help, thinks Raffy, as he does look quite old. He wouldn't be much use in an argument or a punch-up, though.

'You come with me, Colette,' says Raffy. 'You know what it's like. They'll let girls in when they won't let blokes in, sexist pigs.'

He takes Colette's hand and they push and shove their way to the back of the pub. As they get nearer, the noise becomes deafening. At the doorway into the back room, they are stopped by two huge bouncers. A woman is sitting at a small table with a little lamp. She has bleached blonde hair and tattoos on her arms.

'You a member?' she grunts to Raffy.

'I might be,' smiles Raffy. 'I'm in so many clubs.'

'You're not in this one,' says the woman. 'So piss off.'

Raffy looks inside the room. It is so crowded that people have to stand still, unable to move. Most of them look as if they don't want to move, anyway. They are blank, expressionless, dead. On stage, a sub-metal group is working itself into a lather, especially the lead singer. He is writhing on the floor, punching the stage, punching out his words as if they have enormous meaning, though not one of them can be heard.

'Move your arse,' says the woman.

'Actually,' begins Raffy, 'we have some very important French visitors with us. They represent a college of a thousand students who might all be coming –'

'Move, I said,' says the woman. 'Or I'll move you.'

'Okay,' says Raffy. 'I'll join. How much?'

'We're full,' says the woman. 'Mick, sort out this shithouse.'

Then her face suddenly breaks into a wide smile. She is human after all, thinks Raffy. And quite young.

'Colette,' she says, standing up to reveal she's only five feet nothing, leaning over and smiling. 'Lovely to see you.'

'Oh, hi,' says Colette, peering closer, trying to work out who she is.

'How's your mum, then?'

'Oh, fine, fine.'

'If I'd known it was you . . .' says the woman. 'You can come in, but not this jerk.'

'Oh, thanks,' says Colette, 'but we're in a party. They're waiting for us. We're going on somewhere. Thanks anyway.'

Raffy drags her away. As they push through the crowd by the bar, he asks her who the woman was.

'Angela,' says Colette. 'She has the flat above us. She's a primary-school teacher. Least, she used to be.'

Back at the bar, Raffy tells the others it's hopeless. The place is full. No admission possible.

'Good,' says Jules. 'Then we can go to your place, Taz. Cocoa or coffee, hmm, *mes copains*?'

The French all look disappointed. They slowly follow Jules and Taz out of the pub and along the pavement, stepping round all the litter, walking towards Hampstead in the direction of Taz's home.

A taxi screeches to a halt beside them. The rear

door opens and a young executive type in a smart suit jumps out.

'Quick, get in,' he says. 'Three of you in here, beside Blanche. Hurry up, we haven't got all night.

'Driver, radio for another cab. And make it quick. It's on the account, of course: TPR Marketing. Come on, you lot, get in.'

'Dim?' says Colette. 'What are you doing?'

'Don't ask questions. Just get in . . .'

A Mayfair nightclub, much, much later that evening

The group of friends, including Dim and Blanche, are sitting at a large table in a very smart nightclub, deep in Mayfair. They have had a meal and unlimited drinks, on the house, and now the cabaret is about to begin.

Raffy did worry about his jeans, wishing he'd put on a clean pair. Luckily, though, he has got on a neckerchief, which looks slightly more respectable than his usual unadorned T-shirt. Colette dressed up for the evening, knowing she was going out somewhere, though not expecting anywhere as posh as this. Taz and Jules – well, they can go anywhere, any time, as they always look well smart.

'But who's paying for all this?' asks Colette.

'Col, my darling,' says Dim, 'just trust your old friend.'

'Come on, Dim,' says Raffy. 'Don't mess around. What's the secret?'

'No secret,' says Dim. 'All you have to do is remember that all of yous are members of the

78

Sixth-Form Committee, if my old friend Mr Franklin drops in, okay? That means you lot don't say a word.'

Dim smiles at the French contingent. They have absolutely no idea what is going on, but it doesn't worry them. They assume this is what usually happens when you're in London.

'Okay, dim dim,' says Blanche. She takes Dim's hand and presses his fingers against her lips. Raffy and Colette both try to look the other way.

'You can talk now, my blankety blank,' says Dim to Blanche.

'Oh good,' says Blanche. 'Well, I just want to thank you, Dim, for everything. And all of you.'

'What have you liked best?' asks Dim. 'Apart from me . . .'

'The people,' says Blanche.

'What people?' asks Colette.

'Just all the people. They are so different.'

'It is true,' says Pierre. 'English people are so, how you say, original. They look different with one another. You see every kind here. When we were in Covent Garden, or your Camden Lock, or on the tube, we keep seeing people who are different. In Paris, most people looks the same.'

'We just liked looking at people,' says Didier. 'That was the best thing.'

'God, we should just have sent you photographs,' says Raffy. 'You'd have saved all your money.'

'You didn't go on the tube, did you?' says Taz, horrified.

'Yes, it was wonderful,' says Jean-Louis.

'But it's horrible,' says Kirsty, holding Jean-Louis's hand under the table. 'Especially the Northern Line, the one I took you on.'

'It was good,' says Jean-Louis. 'Easier to understand to the Paris Métro.'

'And we liked all the clothes places,' says Blanche. 'That's all I've brought. Three dresses and six scarves.'

'Yes,' says Pierre. 'And that was the first day only.'

'I got Levis,' says Didier. 'Half the price of Paris.'

'But what about the filth of London?' asks Jules.

'You mean the language?' asks Blanche. 'I like the language. Tomorrow I'm going to say to Monsieur Condom, "You are a f— dum dum."'

'I mean the litter and rubbish everywhere,' says Jules. 'The graffiti. The vandalism. Everyone in Britain complains about the state of London streets.'

'We didn't notice,' says Blanche. 'It all looked okay to us.'

She stares at the other French kids. They shake their heads.

'No, I suppose we were just looking at the people,' says Jean-Louis. 'Especially some people.'

'Pass the sick bag,' says Raffy.

'What is that?' asks Blanche.

'I'll tell you in Paris,' says Raffy. 'When Dim isn't there. It's very rude.'

'There is only one thing we have not seen which I wanted to have seen,' says Blanche.

'Hey, that was a good sentence,' says Raffy.

'Shurrup, dum dum,' says Blanche.

'What's that, Blanche?' asks Taz.

'Lay dee dee.'

'You what?' asks Kirsty.

'Do you mean "la di da"?' says Colette. 'Like posh people speak? Well, this is the place. They're all la di da at the other tables.'

'No, lay dee dee,' says Blanche. 'Every French person wants to meet lay dee dee.'

'Dim, my dear chap! So there you are.' A tall man in a dinner jacket has suddenly materialized at their table. 'No, don't get up. How are you all enjoying it?'

'Oh, fine, thanks,' says Dim, who has stood up, being ever so polite. 'This is Mr Franklin. These are all the members of our Sixth-Form Committee.'

'Yes, I've heard all about you and your magnificent work. Jolly good. Anyway, don't let me interrupt. Hey, you're not drinking much wine. Do order some more. And don't forget it's on the bill, just sign for TPR Marketing. I'll hear from you on Monday evening, Dim. Then we'll really get down to the nitty gritty.'

When Mr Franklin has gone back to another party in the far corner of the club, everyone stares at Dim.

'What is going on here?' asks Jules.

'It's a new club,' says Dim. 'I think his firm's executives have all got free membership, just to get the place going.'

'Yeah, but the food and booze . . .' says Raffy. 'Who's paying?'

'You heard,' says Dim. 'TPR Marketing.'

'What's that?' asks Kirsty.

'Tufnell Park Rubber,' says Dim. 'They are going to install the condom machines in our sixth-form bogs.'

'But we haven't got agreement yet,' says Colette.

'They know that. I'll give them a definite yes or no on Monday night. I've played fair with them. They know the score.'

'But there's no score,' says Colette. 'Not yet.'

'Toby and Ella think there will be,' says Dim, patiently. 'They've nobbled the parent governors. I mean, persuaded them. I've been over it all with several firms in this line of business. They all loved it. I've been wined and dined for two weeks. It's been pretty exhausting.'

'Poor Dim,' says Raffy. 'Why didn't you say? I could have helped.'

'I had to keep it quiet till I chose one firm, after consulting Ella and Toby. I wanted to tell Colette, but she didn't seem, I dunno, very interested.'

'Oh, I would have been,' says Colette.

'TPR are the keenest,' continues Dim. 'They've got plans for marketing, with ads in the colour mags, perhaps on TV as well. They'll show us in our common room, all looking serious, with just a glimpse of one of their machines in the background. They're even planning a new brand, aimed at sixth formers, named after us. You know how they name types of football boots after footballers? Well, they're thinking of launching Star-right, or Star-light . . .

'When the national campaign starts, then we'll get paid extra for any modelling we do, personal appearances, TV and radio interviews.'

'Bloody hell, Dim,' says Raffy.

'Yes, after Monday,' says Dim, 'it could all be very big business indeed.'

'Oh God, we'll miss all the excitement,' says Raffy, genuinely regretful. 'We'll be in Paris.'

'Never mind,' says Dim. 'Drink up. The night's young, the bill is paid for. What do you think of it so far, Blanche?'

'Not rubb-eesh.'

Colette: thinking of Dim

EPISODE 8

Dover, early Monday morning

Taz, Colette, Jules, Raffy and the other four sixth formers, plus Mrs Ainley, are all exhausted. They got up very early and the train ride has been very bumpy.

'I feel rotten,' says Raffy, as the train approaches the station at Dover. 'I think we should have waited longer before setting off. Till the Channel Tunnel was completed.'

Mrs Ainley smiles. Most teachers have learned never to smile at Raffy's jokes. It just encourages him. But she has been in great good humour ever since the French exchange started.

'I've got shares in the tunnel,' she says. 'Least, my husband bought them for us.' She pauses and a slight frown crosses her face. 'I think half of them are in my name.'

'You capitalist pig,' says Colette. 'Wait till I tell Dim. He'll want you to re-invest them in this scheme of his – er, I mean, something different.'

'It was just an amusement really,' says Mrs Ainley, half to herself. 'If you bought them at the beginning, you get a free ride the year the tunnel opens.'

They walk from the train across to the harbour proper. Then Raffy and the others stand and stare in amazement at the large, round object, stranded just ahead of them. It lies on a clump of concrete like an enormous jellyfish, its rubber tentacles flopping all around it.

'Is it a bird?' exclaims Raffy. 'Is it a fish? Is it a plane?' He pretends to play a trumpet, blowing a fanfare. Some of the other sixth formers are already wishing Raffy had never chosen to take French. Or had chosen an exchange in French West Africa.

'No, folks, it's a space ship!'

They eventually get aboard the hovercraft and settle down. Once it starts off, they pronounce it dead good, well smart, discussing amongst themselves whether it is more like a plane because of the flight number, the seats, hostesses and the fact that it rose in the air at take-off time, or more like a boat because of the way it skims over the waves.

'Don't think much of the driver,' says Raffy. 'Or should that be pilot. My stomach has gone missing, with him swerving all over the place.'

'How do you know it's a man?' asks Taz.

'Good thinking. Only a woman driver could steer like this. Oh, I feel terrible.'

'You shouldn't have started on your bottle of duty free,' says Colette.

'Just checking it out,' says Raffy. 'It's for Didier's parents. I hope yous have all brought presents. How about you, Lizzie? You got something nice for Monsieur Condom, apart from *le nudge nudge*? You should have got him a bottle of Teachers, ha ha.'

'We'll all be too busy working hard this week for any drinking,' smiles Mrs Ainley. 'Or nudging.'

'Oh yeah?' says Raffy. 'I've told you, I see this week as a holiday. Just as they did. What a load of skivers they were, bunking off school all the time. Must be Liberty Hall at their *lycée*.'

'I think you'll be rather surprised,' says Mrs Ainley.

'I'm terrified,' says Colette. 'I've decided I can't talk French at all. When they all talked to each other, I couldn't understand a word.'

'Yeah, I found that,' says Raffy. 'I prefer talking French to English-speaking people. The British speak French much more clearly than the French, don't you agree? They can certainly understand me much better. Who needs France? In fact, let's get off now. Race you back to the white cliffs of Dover . . .'

'It's just like a bleedin' foreign language, when they all start,' says Colette.

Mrs Ainley bursts out laughing this time. Colette is not quite aware of what she has just said.

'Yes, you're in for some surprises,' adds Mrs Ainley.

Gare du Nord railway station, Paris

There is no school minibus to pick the English party up, but almost all the exchange partners are there, and Monsieur Condom, plus several parents with cars. At once, it is kisses and hugs all round, even though they have been apart only a few days. Monsieur Condom appears ecstatic to see Mrs Ainley.

Colette and Raffy find themselves in the same car, a Renault Espace, along with Jean-Louis and Didier. Didier's mother is driving. She is very tall, wears cowboy boots, smokes non-stop and insists on talking non-stop while driving, turning round all the time and pointing out landmarks to Raffy and Colette. Raffy prides himself on keeping his end up in any language and any company, but he soon finds his jaw beginning to ache, trying to look interested, and his ears throbbing, trying to understand.

It takes Didier's mother about forty minutes to reach Asnières, just on the outskirts of the city, during which time she has given them a potted history of Paris. Or it could have been Outer Mongolia, for all Colette has understood.

'Where are we?' Colette whispers to Jean-Louis. 'I mean, "*Où sommes nous?*"'

'Nearly there,' says Jean-Louis. 'That block on the corner, you see? That's where Monsieur Condom lives.'

'Is he – er – married?' asks Raffy.

'No,' says Jean-Louis. 'We all thought he might

87

be – how do you say – jolly? Till last week in London. Now we're not so sure.'

'What happened?' says Raffy. 'And have you got pictures? I could use them in my next article for the mag.'

'We don't know,' says Jean-Louis. 'It's Blanche who is saying these things. And, as you know, Blanche does like to talk rubbeesh. Especially when she is *un peu* pissed.'

'What eeze "peesed"?' asks Didier's mother. 'It is rain?'

'*Oui, maman,*' says Didier.

'Ah yes,' says Didier's mother, 'eet rains a lot in London, no?'

Jean-Louis's house

Colette and Jean-Louis have been dropped off on the pavement with their bags by Didier's mother. Colette feels there must be some mistake. The street is more like an empty railway siding, with not a house in sight, just a long, dirty, brick wall, covered with fading but once-garish advertisements for soap powder and posters announcing long-gone concerts. She notices that one concert was given by the Pogues.

'Er, this is not a trick is it, Jean-Louis?' she says. She has been warming to him since they arrived. He seems nicer on his home territory than in London, but then, he was chasing Kirsty all the time there. Or avoiding her mother.

'A trick?'

'Yeah, you know, I'll wake up in South America.'

He smiles and leads the way to a grey, wooden door in the wall, which she had not noticed before. He takes out a key and opens it, beckoning her to go through. '*Entrez, mademoiselle.*'

'*Merci, m'sieur,*' says Colette. 'Right, that's my French exhausted now.'

She finds herself in a small, enclosed courtyard, covered in vines, shrubs and wisteria. At one side is a small, three-storey cottage, with a red tiled roof and blue shutters.

'Hey, it's pretty neat,' says Colette.

'Well, it is not as big as some of your London houses,' says Jean-Louis. 'Not like Sam's. But it is not usual, for Paris. Most of my friends live in apartments.'

They go inside, where Jean-Louis's mother gives Colette a kiss on both cheeks. She is small, thin, bird-like, but smartly dressed. She takes Colette to her room.

'You have this to yourself,' she says, in excellent English, much to Colette's relief. 'It is your room. Sorry it is so small.' Colette wonders if Jean-Louis's mother is making some reference to their titchy flat in London.

The room is in the attic, with a bare wooden floor, a very low ceiling and simple but attractive furniture.

'Oh, it's lovely,' says Colette.

'We'll be having supper soon,' says Jean-Louis's mother, leaving the room. 'Come below when you are ready.'

Colette starts to unpack. She stops suddenly

when she hears a dreadful moaning and groaning coming through the wall. Then a lot of crashing and banging.

'Is it Jean-Louis?' she thinks, alarmed. 'No, he told me his room is in the basement. Hmm. So they're keeping us apart, eh?'

Then she hears spitting and choking. She wonders if someone is locked up, a prisoner in the other part of the attic. Is Jean-Louis really a schoolboy after all? Where is this house? *Could* it be South America?

'I want my mummy,' says Colette out loud, just to amuse herself, and to let this strange person through the wall know that someone new has arrived.

Didier's home

Didier lives in a small flat in a modern block. Not unlike the tower block where Kirsty lives, thinks Raffy. But as it's France, with different smells, different sounds and sights, it feels quite exotic. There's also a lot more washing hanging out of the windows and balconies than you'd find in London.

Raffy is standing in Didier's bedroom, which he is going to share, a room about the same size as his own back in London. Didier has gone back into the living room to watch television, leaving Raffy to unpack.

'I could have had him to stay with me at home after all,' thinks Raffy. 'There's as much space here as my gran's flat. I shouldn't have been ashamed.

And my gran would have loved it. Spoiled him rotten, she would.'

He looks round the bedroom at the books and posters, magazines and comics, especially the comics. There do seem to be a lot of those.

'David Bowie! Bloody hell's teeth,' says Raffy, opening a cupboard and looking at the photographs and posters pinned up inside the door.

He makes a space in the wardrobe and hangs up his clothes. He was going to have a shower, but decides not to brave the funny-looking contraption. Then, taking out a clean shirt, he examines some clean underpants. He's brought five pairs, one for each day of the visit, which is going it a bit. He usually makes them last two days at home, but he is on location, after all, hoping to do some shooting.

Raffy holds up two pairs of his underpants, trying to decide between the boxer shorts, which are now out of fashion, or the new-style Y-fronts, which are bang in fashion. Or at least they were eight hours ago, when he left London.

'But will the Frogettes know that? Will I be casting pearls before *cochons*? Oh well, let's stun them with the Y-fronts. Give the Parisian girls a thrill.'

Raffy takes off his clothes, singing to himself. 'Oh, you ain't seen nothing yet, tra la.' The bedroom door quietly opens while he is still singing, half-naked. He suddenly realizes Didier's mother is watching him in the cupboard mirror. She is still in her big cowboy boots, but is now wearing stretch jeans, rather too tight, and a low-cut, frilly blouse.

'Oh, my good God,' thinks Raffy. 'Stick 'em up,' he says, pulling on his jeans, then turning round.

'Pardon me?' says Didier's mother. 'Stick up what?'

'Just a joke,' says Raffy, becoming almost embarrassed, a strange sensation for him. 'You looked a bit like "Annie get your gun".'

'I just wanted to say –' says Didier's mother, sitting down on Raffy's bed and watching him carefully, smoking a cigarette, as ever.

'Yes?' says Raffy.

'There is another bedroom next door . . .'

'Great,' says Raffy, dreading what might be coming next, getting the rest of his clothes on as quickly as possible. 'That's nice.'

'But there is no need to go into it,' says Didier's mother. 'Is that understood, hmmm?'

'*Bien sûr*,' says Raffy, rather relieved. 'Anyway, I think I'll hardly be here. We're invited to Blanche's later on. That's supposed to be where all the action is. Then, of course, it will be school every day. Work work, work. 'Scuse me.' He squeezes past the bed, from which Didier's mother is still watching his every movement, and goes into the living room for his first experience of French television.

Jean-Louis's, suppertime

Colette is starting her first course, some sort of shellfish. They look like mussels, which she quite likes when her mother buys them ready-prepared, at Mark's and Spencer. But these mussels have been cooked in a funny way, or so Colette thinks, with strange herbs and bits and pieces floating amongst them.

Jean-Louis has already half-finished his, making a disgusting noise as he dips huge hunks of bread in the juice, then lifts up the bowl to suck down every drop. His mother tells him off, but he ignores her.

She is being kind to Colette, looking after her, speaking mostly in English to her. Jean-Louis's father speaks very little English. He did try at first, saying 'How are you?' 'Okay', 'No problem', but soon gave up and is now looking very bored.

Suddenly, the sound of loud banging comes from above, on the ceiling. The noise of shuffling steps can be heard, coming down the wooden staircase, followed by great coughs and splutters. The three French people stop eating, look at each other, raise their eyebrows and sigh. A very old, dirty-looking man staggers into the room, cursing and swearing. Colette presumes he must be swearing, as Jean-Louis's mother makes a remark which sounds like a reprimand. The old man's accent and his moustache are so thick that she can't understand a word. He pulls out a chair beside Colette and drops into it, scattering his napkin and cutlery, which Jean-Louis's mother rushes to pick up.

'This is my father,' she explains to Colette. 'He stays with us all years from Easter to October, then he lives with my sister in the Midi. Don't let him upset you.'

'Of course not,' says Colette, looking worried. 'He looks very nice.'

'Don't lie,' says Jean-Louis. 'He's a pig.'

Colette turns to smile at Jean-Louis, but finds herself being tugged at by his grandfather. He is spluttering right over her, his mouth full of bread and yellowing teeth, shouting something at her in French. The longer she takes to understand, the louder he shouts, getting angrier and angrier.

Jean-Louis's mother tells him off, in French, then gets up and passes him the wine.

'Oh God,' says Colette. 'Was that all it was? *"Passez-moi du vin."* And I couldn't even understand a simple phrase like that. God, I'm so hopeless. I'll never learn anything.'

'Of course you will, my dear,' says the mother.

The grandfather has now turned to Jean-Louis, shouting at him, for some reason. Jean-Louis shouts back till they are both yelling, waving their hands, making faces, spluttering and gesticulating. All Colette can make out is the word *stupide*.

'Why is he being stupid?' she asks Jean-Louis's mother.

'They're both stupid. Jean-Louis makes him angry, so my father makes battles by calling him stupid, which he is so. He had had to resit a year at school, so whenever they have argument, my father says this to him.'

'Resit a year?'

'Yes, it's quite usual in France, especially in the lower years. About a third of people have to do it. *Redoublement*, we call it.'

'So that's why he's older than the rest of the

class,' says Colette. 'We all thought he was a teacher when we first saw him.'

'He should like that.'

'God, I hope they won't make me resit anything this week,' says Colette. 'I've got to get home to my mother on Saturday.'

Blanche's home, later that evening

Colette, Raffy and Jules are whispering to Taz, telling her how lucky she is to be in this lovely place. Not that they don't like where they are, but all the same, Blanche's place is clearly the smartest. She and Taz have obviously been matched together as they both come from similarly affluent homes.

'Just like you, Taz,' says Colette. 'You've drawn the long straw. Jules, what's that in French, huh?'

Blanche lives in a flat, not a house, but it is in a nineteenth-century block, old but posh, with an imposing entrance hall, a Portuguese *concierge*, wide corridors and massive rooms with ornate ceilings. The flat itself seems to have at least ten rooms. Taz has not explored them all yet, but those she has seen are beautifully decorated and furnished, and usually buzzing with people. Blanche's parents are arty types, both successful writers. But very clean, so Taz adds in her card home. The flat is near to the *lycée* and, like Sam's house in London, is the meeting place for all Blanche's friends. They are always welcome, at all hours.

Blanche has a large room at the back of the flat, in the well of the building. One wall is made completely from glass, and the room looks like an indoor conservatory, as it has lots of plants growing everywhere.

'My brudder,' Blanche is explaining, 'was used to grow special plants in here, you understand? But my father, he find out. I think he takes them for himself.'

She gives her deep, throaty laugh, taking another drag on her cigarette. All the other French kids, especially the girls, are smoking as well. Jules, Taz and Colette do not smoke at all, so they are finding the atmosphere rather fuggy. Even Raffy feels it. He does smoke, a little, but only on social occasions, which means when other people are providing the means. He has been offered a cigarette, but doesn't like French ones. He is saving himself for the booze which he is sure will appear soon, as Blanche's family are obviously well-off.

The stereo is on, loudly. So far, the music has all been British, most of it at least two years old, plus a few American groups.

'It's the same everywhere,' says Colette. 'Have you noticed? I haven't heard any French pop music yet.'

'It is all rubbeesh, that's why,' says Blanche. 'London is better.'

'So what is it you are wanting to do in Paris?' asks Pierre, turning to the English partners.

'I'd love to go to a fashion show,' says Jules.

'What a poser,' groans Raffy.

'What is a "poser"?' asks Blanche.

'Jules,' says Raffy.

'I understand,' says Blanche.

'I'd like to see the Eiffel Tower,' says Colette. 'The Champs-Elysées, Montmartre, Versailles and, oh yes, the Beaubourg thingy,' says Colette.

'Oh, Gordon Bennet,' says Raffy.

'Where is this Gordon?' asks Didier. 'It is a new building?'

'I'll tell you in bed tonight,' says Raffy. 'If you're good.'

'I'd like to visit the clothes shops in the Faubourg St-Honoré,' says Taz.

'You are all so superficial,' says Raffy. 'No higher aspirations than the obvious. I dunno.'

'So tell me, darling. What are your plans, Raffy?' says Blanche.

'At the moment,' says Raffy, 'very simple. I'd like to get pissed, then after that, a *morceau de legover, s'il vous plaît.*'

'I understand part of that now, anyway,' says Blanche. 'So let's go . . .'

Later, in a local Parisian street

'This is it,' says Blanche, leading the way. 'It just has opened. We have not been yet. We are saving it, just for you.'

She leads the way through a brightly painted doorway into a well-lit bar, with posters on the wall.

'Quite nice,' says Colette politely.

'Hold on,' says Raffy, looking round the walls. 'I recognize those views.'

The posters show the Tower of London, beef-eaters, Buckingham Palace, British bobbies and a London double-decker bus. Behind the bar, mine host is sporting an RAF moustache, a club tie, a Viyella shirt and a sports jacket. Above his head are corny sayings written in English on bits of wood. 'You don't have to be stupid to work here, but it helps.'

'It is *le English Pub*,' says Blanche, delighted with herself.

The English students all look at each other, but no one has the heart to say anything. Not even 'Rubbish.'

'Let me get you drinks,' says Blanche, going over to the bar and ordering in English, without even asking them what they want. She returns with a Whitbread tray, loaded with bottles of lukewarm Pale Ale, plus some Babychams.

Raffy groans, but Colette kicks him. They all dutifully drink their drinks.

'Actually, Blanche,' says Colette, 'I'm knackered. You know, exhausted. Been a long day. I think I'll get to bed early.'

'What about *le legover*, whatever that is?'

'I'll save my legs,' says Raffy, 'for another evening.'

Even Raffy is tired. And when a raver is tired of Paris, is he tired of life?

Taz: taking a break

EPISODE 9

Lycée, Friday morning

Taz, Colette, Jules and Raffy are in an English class.
It is being taken by Monsieur Condom. He wears
glasses for lessons and looks very fierce. They have
been in his class several times this week and most of
the time have been unable to understand what's
been going on – despite the fact that he's been
teaching English. And often *in* English.

One problem has been grammar, about which
the English students appear to know very little.
Even though it's their own language, and even
though Monsieur Condom uses English words like
subjunctive, past participle, adverb, gerund, active
and passive. All week he has given them examples
of each condition when it has cropped up in his

lessons, yet they still don't appear to know what he's talking about. The foreign language in this case is English.

'Be so good as to tell us, Mr Raphael, what the difference is between an ode and a sonnet,' says Monsieur Condom, suddenly turning on Raffy, just when he was hoping to doze off.

'We don't do no grammar,' replies Raffy cheekily, but not quite as cheekily as he might have replied back home in his own school.

'We don't do *any* grammar,' corrects Monsieur Condom. 'Lesson fifteen, paragraph five. Class, now turn to it.'

The whole class, except Raffy, dutifully open their textbooks.

'Yeah, but in conversation, that's what we'd say,' says Raffy, slightly on the defensive. He's not used to his own wordpower, his own language, being under attack. 'Obviously I wouldn't use that phrase in an essay or an exam.'

'Why not?'

'Cos it's wrong.'

'Why is it wrong?'

'I dunno,' says Raffy. 'You tell me.' Under his breath he adds 'Clever clogs', but not loud enough to be heard.

'Two negatives make an affirmative,' says Monsieur Condom, 'so you are saying the opposite of what you intend to say. Thonat, give me another example, in English, of two negatives.'

Blanche stands up to answer. This is one of the many classroom customs that completely amazed the English. For a start, there are forty students in the class, as opposed to no more than a dozen in their lower sixth classes at home. Everyone sits at a little desk, in rows, and they are made to learn things parrot fashion, by rote, followed up by endless written tests.

'I don't like no rubbish,' says Blanche.

'Thank you, Thonat,' says Monsieur Condom, as Blanche sits down.

That's another surprise. Most of the teachers address all the pupils, even girls, by their surnames. In return, all pupils use the form *vous* when talking to teachers, the impersonal plural, rather than the *tu* form they would use with their friends. Raffy has listened carefully all week and it's only in a conversation with a gym teacher that he has heard *tu* being used. But then, gym teachers everywhere are different. Sometimes for the better, sometimes for the worse. But they're usually different.

Monsieur Condom returns to his question about the difference between an ode and a sonnet. When that has been established, with Didier's help, they are told to get out their Wordsworth books. Monsieur Condom then makes them turn the texts over, face down on their desks. At random, he picks on various pupils to recite the sonnet on Westminster Bridge, line by line.

Raffy exchanges looks with Taz and Jules, turning his eyes heavenwards. In London, all the French exchanges raved about the English teaching methods, amazed by the informality, the relaxed style of the teachers, the easy classroom atmosphere, so easy that in the end they did not bother to turn up. Now the English pupils know why. Raffy tried to skive off a couple of the lessons they were timetabled to attend this week by sleeping in, but Didier's mother kept on hanging around his bedroom. He eventually decided he would be safer at the *lycée*.

Monsieur Condom has kept them all up to the mark, sending notes to Mrs Ainley about any late-comers or shirkers, and in turn, Mrs Ainley has asked her pupils to be good, just for the rest of their stay, to please Monsieur Condom and help good relations between the two schools. French teachers, so she has told them, do not have a high opinion of English comprehensive-school attainment levels. For example, twice as many pupils in France get through their *baccalauréat* as English pupils pass their A levels, the rough equivalent, and then go on to further education. France does have something to boast about, so Mrs Ainley has told them.

Monsieur Condom is now waxing lyrically about his own memories of standing on Westminster Bridge as a young student, an *assistant*. He explains how Wordsworth was expressing great pride in his country, thinking of London's greatness.

'No, he wasn't,' says Raffy. 'He was thinking of his French mistress.'

The whole class turns and looks at Raffy, stunned. Not just by the fact that he has so rudely interrupted a teacher in full flow, but by what he has said.

'I beg your pardon?' says Monsieur Condom.

'Yeah, well, he got this French bird up the spout – know what I mean, in the family way – and she has this kid, right, by him, illegitimate and all that, then he buggers off back to England. Years later, when he's about to get married to his English girlfriend, he decides to go to France and tell his old mistress what he's gonna do. He's on the way to Boulogne to see her when he crosses Westminster Bridge and thinks up this poem.'

'Calais, actually,' says Taz.

'Yeah, that's right,' says Raffy. 'I did a project on it last year, for GCSE, "Wordsworth's Sex Life". I'll send yous copies if you like.'

Several of the pupils are writing notes in their workbooks, but Monsieur Condom tells them to stop. 'I don't think you will need that sort of material in your exams,' he says. 'It's not exactly relevant.'

'Oh, it is,' says Jules. 'There is a school of thought which claims that there is no real passion in Wordsworth's poems, of a sensual or sexual nature, because there was none in his life.'

'In fact,' says Taz, 'it was a Frenchman, Emile Legouis, who first wrote about Wordsworth's French girlfriend. You can't really understand *The Prelude* unless you know all about that.'

The bell goes before Monsieur Condom can reply. Nobody moves till he tells them to, then the pupils obediently file out, one by one, quietly and sedately.

Le foyer, lunchtime

Raffy, Jules, Taz, Colette and their French friends

are relaxing in their lunch break after a hard morning's work. Some of them are eating. Some are reading. Some are looking at *les devoirs*, or homework. Didier is turning over the pages of his exercise book, explaining the marking system to Taz.

'What's TB mean?' she asks.

'That stands for *très bien*,' says Didier. 'Usually it means seventeen or more out of twenty.'

'Of course,' says Taz.

'*Bien* means about fifteen out of twenty. *Assez bien* is thirteen. A pass in any exam is ten out of twenty. We call that *la moyenne*.'

'I see,' says Taz.

'Give us a break, Taz,' says Raffy. 'Wouldn't you like something else to eat and drink, huh? I'm starving.'

'We have had *un sandwich* or *un hamburger à la cantine*,' says Jules, 'and we are now in *le foyer* where people are playing *au football*. Tell me, don't you have any French words in the French language these days?'

Blanche and the others laugh. 'It really pisses away the older generation,' says Blanche, 'all these English words creeping in. But we like it. We all want to know the latest.'

'Hold on,' says Taz, opening her new leather handbag from the Avenue Montaigne and getting out her dictionary. 'I bet *foyer* was originally French and we've pinched it from them. I'll just look it up.'

'Oh, my good God,' says Colette. 'We're not in

the classroom now. I'm knackered. I dunno how you lot stand all this learning. You don't start every day at eight o'clock, do you?'

'Yes,' says Didier. 'Till four-thirty. Sometimes till five-thirty, if we have extra work. And we come in on Saturday mornings as well.'

'God, better you than me,' says Raffy, getting out a can of beer from his *Bon Marché* carrier bag. All the French students immediately jump on him, shouting at him to put it away.

'Stop it,' says Pierre. 'You can't drink here.'

'Then where can I drink?' asks Raffy. 'You don't have anywhere to yourself in this place. You should go on strike, you know, to get your own common room. I thought our school was bad, but this is ridiculous. Is this really all you've got?'

He gestures round at *le foyer*. As the name suggests, it is simply a large entrance hall, used by the whole *lycée*. The football being played is table football, though the real wasters and ravers can also play *au ping-pong*.

'This is all,' says Blanche. 'Rubb-eesh, ain't it, mate?'

'I'll go into the playground and drink there then,' says Raffy.

'No, you can't,' says Didier.

'But people smoke in your playground. Why can't you drink?'

'It's just the rules,' says Pierre.

'God, it's like a prison,' says Colette. 'You're not allowed to do anything.'

'Yes, you are so lucky,' says Blanche. 'I wish I

went to an English school. I like your lessons better as well.'

'Was that a joke, about Wordsworth's sex life?' asks Didier.

'All true,' says Raffy. 'It was one of my projects.'

Jules then explains about projects and course-work, how written exams in England are often only a minor part of public examinations, and how there is great freedom to choose what you study, though it has to be agreed with your teacher.

'The theory now,' says Taz, 'is that you should be tested on what you know, on what you can do, rather than on what you don't know, or can't do.'

'Oh, that's much better,' says Blanche. 'We'll probably do that in about a hundred years' time. Jean-ai Condom is so old-fashioned.'

'Who?' asks Taz.

'It's our little joke,' says Blanche. 'We call him *J'en ai* Condom, instead of Jean. Understand?'

'Hey, that's very good,' says Jules. 'The only trouble is, I'll never be able to explain it in Camden Town.'

'We are about to change soon,' says Didier. 'Our education minister is going to make lessons not so strict, and stop the *redoublement* system. They're all arguing about it now. It's written in the news-papers.'

'They're also arguing in England,' says Taz. 'There's a move to bring back formal teaching, with tests at every stage. We could end up being taught like you are now, and you'll end up like us.'

'*C'est la vie*,' says Colette. ''Scuse my French.'

'You mean *toilette*,' says Raffy. 'It's rude to say lavvy.' This joke takes a long time for him to explain. He's been making what he thinks are clever bi-lingual puns all week, but no one understand them.

'So, what are we doing this evening then, folks?' says Raffy. 'Last night, and all that.'

'We are making a surprise for you,' says Didier. 'But it is going to be later than we wanted.'

'Why's that?' asks Colette.

'I've been found smoking in a classroom,' says Blanche.

'You what?' says Colette.

'I have to stay behind an hour this evening and sweep the *lycée*. They are all peegs.'

'Bloody hell,' says Raffy, thinking of his can of beer. 'It'll probably be the guillotine if I'm caught drinking in school.'

'But no sweating,' says Blanche. 'No problem. All of you are coming to my place at eight o'clock?'

'*D'accord*,' says Colette.

'No, I think we'll probably walk,' says Raffy.

Jean-Louis's home, early evening

The family is having supper. Colette is trying not to eat very much, as she is looking forward to enjoying whatever surprise is being organized for their last evening. She has asked Jean-Louis several times for details. He says it's a secret, but there will be food available. None the less, he is stuffing himself.

'Are you in an eating competition?' Colette says

to him. 'Trying to get into the French team for eating?'

'All Frenchmen are in the team for eating,' says Jean-Louis's mother. 'It's the favourite game.'

She gets up and brings in the pudding, which she says is just something simple. It turns out to be homemade pancakes, stuffed with some delicious filling and dripping with hot chocolate. Colette succumbs at once.

'I do like French chocolate,' she says, tucking in. 'It's sort of bitterer and stronger than ours. I'm taking loads home as presents. For my mum of course. And myself . . .'

'Your English chocolate is not real chocolate,' says Madame Adeline. 'It has lots of things extra, like vegetable oils. In France, chocolate must to be made from pure *cacao*, butter and milk.'

'Actually, I like English chocolate more,' says Jean-Louis. 'It's much sweeter. I like artificial things.'

'You have no taste,' says his mother.

Her father starts spluttering and shouting, looking very angry. Madame Adeline explains that he's fed-up with them talking English. He's saying this is France, damn it, or what's left of France now that the Anglo-Saxons are determined to ruin the whole country with their fast food, fast words, ugly fashions and loud music.

He suddenly grabs hold of Colette and starts pulling her hair, holding up strands of it, smelling it, and generally shouting and cursing. Even Jean-Louis is not sure what he's on about this time.

'I think he tells you his biggest compliment,' says Jean-Louis's mother.

'Oh yeah?' says Colette. 'Doesn't sound like it.'

'He's saying you could be quite pretty –'

'Yes?'

'– if only you did something to your hair.'

'Thanks a lot,' says Colette, pulling her hair out of the old man's grasp and giving him a gentle slap on the wrist. 'Just spent a fortune on it, you cheeky bugger. Those highlights weren't cheap.'

The grandfather laughs and slaps the table, spluttering even more, spitting bits of food everywhere. Then he starts muttering again, pointing at Colette.

'What's he on about this time?'

'He says he's got a present for you and your mother. He'll leave it for you tomorrow in the morning.'

'Oh, that is kind,' says Colette. She leans towards him, about to give him a kiss, though not sure if she can bear to. But she manages it. He bursts out laughing, then takes her hand and kisses it.

'We must go to Blanche's house now,' says Jean-Louis, dragging Colette out of her chair. 'Come on. Let us get our skating boots on.'

Didier's flat

Raffy is getting dressed in his best clothes. Very carefully, he puts on the last of his clean underpants. His shirt, unfortunately, is not quite so fresh. It is the one he wore on their day trip to Versailles, and he did sweat a lot in the sun. Then he got Calvados marks on it that night, arm wrestling with Blanche in a bar. She won. To compensate for the stains, Raffy lavishes on even more aftershave than normal. Plus double gel on his hair.

When he is finally ready, he tidies up the bedroom and packs most of his things away, in preparation for an early departure the next day. He closes the bedroom door, then stops in the little hallway, looking at the next door, the door of the room he is not supposed to enter. He listens carefully. Didier and his mother are in the living room, the television blaring.

Slowly, Raffy turns the handle and opens the door. The blinds in the room are closed and at first it appears very dark. When his eyes get used to the light, he sees there is an old desk in one corner, covered in books and papers. A spotlight is trained on one particular book. Behind the desk sits a very thin, worn-looking man, smoking a cigarette, hunched over the book with his head down.

Raffy tries to retreat as quietly as possible, but the man looks up, having seen him.

'*Oui?*' he says. '*Que désirez-vous?*'

'*Oh, rien,*' mutters Raffy. '*Je cherche le téléphone. Excusez-moi.*'

He closes the door quickly, hurries down the corridor and goes into the living room. Having said he wanted the phone and worried in case the strange man follows him, he asks if he may make a call. Didier's mother nods, pointing to the phone in the entrance hall.

Raffy picks the receiver up, not sure who to dial.

He finds himself ringing Dim's home, the minicab number, thinking he might just get the answerphone. Dim himself replies.

'Hi, it's me, Raffy,' he says. 'We're having a brilliant time here. What's new? . . . No! You're joking . . . Honestly? You're not taking the piss? Bloody brilliant . . . Wait till I tell them . . . Yeah, I'm off to meet them all, this minute . . . *Au revoir, mon ami.*'

Blanche's studio room, much, much later that night

The most spectacular party Raffy and Colette have ever attended is in progress. Even Taz and Jules, who pride themselves on having been around the London scene, up West, points South, admit it is amazing. Especially considering that Blanche and her classmates have done the whole thing themselves. Raffy was expecting they would be going out somewhere, possibly to the English pub again, so he is thrilled. All the English kids are. It is their first true taste of the Parsian teenage scene. Over fifty people are present, mostly from Blanche's class.

They have decorated the studio with Union Jacks and Tricolours. There are balloons and streamers hanging from the ceiling, posters on all the walls. They've even managed to get some Arsenal scarves and banners from somewhere, in honour of Raffy, which are hung up beside posters and badges for the Paris St Germain team.

There are tables groaning with food and bottles of every sort of drink, provided by Blanche's parents. Raffy has been eating and drinking since he arrived, but is still finding space for a little more.

'I must stop,' he says to Blanche, taking a handful of small stuffed plover's eggs. 'An *oeuf* is an *oeuf*.'

Blanche smiles. She can at last understand one of his jokes, mainly because it is one he has cracked several times already this evening and probably will again.

The music is very loud, and once again it is mostly British pop music, if slightly dated.

'Great,' says Raffy as a new number comes on. 'My favourite. *Le garçon George, qui chante.*'

He sits down beside Jules, Colette and Taz, who are deep in a serious conversation with Jean-Louis, Pierre and a few others, about the differences between English and French culture.

'But your fashion houses are world-famous,' says Jules. 'They dominate the world.'

'And some of the women I saw in the Faubourg St-Honoré were so chic,' says Taz.

'Yes, but we have been suffocated by our chic,' says Jean-Louis. 'It's all chic, and no style. It's just a uniform, thought up by a few people, to be worn by a small élite. And that's all it is. London is so different.'

'Yes, it amazed us all in London,' says Pierre. 'The young people everywhere, every class, in the street, on the tube, they dress up so good. Like the punks. And not for a party, not to go somewhere.'

'No, they would be going somewhere,' says Colette. 'The DSS probably, to sign on.' She then has to explain about unemployment benefit and the people who fiddle it. They all laugh, except Didier, who gets up and walks away.

Raffy follows him across the room, stopping by the drinks table, although he has had quite a few by now. He watches Didier going to sit on his own. So he takes a whole bottle and sits down beside him, putting an arm round his shoulders.

'How's it going, pal?' Raffy asks.

'Okay,' says Didier.

'Great staying with you,' says Raffy. 'But I'll tell you something funny. At your place tonight, I went into this room by mistake. And there was this bloke sitting at a desk, reading. Excuse me asking, but who was he, like?'

'My father,' says Didier.

'You what?'

'He is unemployed. He was a teacher, but he lost his job after some row. This was a year ago. He is a Communist. He just sits all day in his room, never going out, smoking, reading, writing. Doing nothing.'

'Oh. I'm very sorry,' says Raffy.

'My mother was trying to tell you all this, but she thinks why bother, you don't need to know.'

Suddenly a loud cheer goes up. Two new people have arrived, though Raffy can't see who they are as the room is so crowded. Someone changes the music from almost modern, heavy, British soul to veritable, ancient, circa 1950s bee-bop French jazz. Blanche comes round, pushing people back to make space and saying that the dancing is now about to begin. Clear the floor, please, stand back, make ready for the first performers.

Two people are jiving at enormous speed and with great enthusiasm. They are Mrs Ainley and Monsieur Condom. She is wearing a sixties-style frock, flared out, with a stiffened petticoat underneath. He is in tight black trousers and a polo neck, with sunglasses on instead of his specs.

A huge cheer goes up the moment they finish. They collapse exhausted, clutching each other, both laughing. Only Didier is not clapping.

A Parisian street, six o'clock in the morning

A giant green snail is slithering down the street. From its underbelly, tubes and suckers snake out, shovelling and siphoning, washing and brushing, blowing and bellowing. The top of this metallic monster then opens and out spring strange beings in green tunics with fluorescent stripes round their shoulders and waists.

'Oh, my good God!' screams Colette in genuine alarm.

'It's the end of the world,' shouts Raffy, equally horrified. 'They've landed. We're being invaded.'

It has been a long night. It is also true to say that Raffy and Colette, and their friends, have been drinking and indulging themselves for some considerable time. All the same, even the native Parisians are slightly startled when they come across these giant contraptions in the early morning, these monsters of *propreté*, going about their job of cleaning up the streets of Paris.

No sooner has the first machine done its watery work than a second appears, known as *le crabe*. A monster bulldozer with a huge cage of a mouth which crunches whole edifices in its jaws, chewing up wood, metal, paper and rotting vegetable matter. Then a third machine, even bigger and commonly called *la benne*, lumbers into the street and waits. The crab, its horror-film work done, spews out all its intestinal garbage into the waiting cavernous hold of its big sister.

'God, it's scary,' says Raffy.

'I want my mum,' says Colette.

The four English students are holding on to each other. Their eyes and ears, assaulted enough over the past few hours, have never seen or heard such a spectacle. It takes them some time to understand what is happening, convinced there must be a hidden meaning or some secret symbolism behind this ritual. Perhaps it is part of a fiendish test set by their once-formidable, though now user-friendly, adversary, the one and only Monsieur Jean Condom.

'Where's André Gide?' says Jules. 'Just when we need him.'

'No, we want Sartre,' says Taz. 'He would explain everything to us.'

Then they all start laughing, splashing in the little pools of water. They are on the way to a café which opens early, where Blanche says they do the best fresh croissants in all Paris.

'I can't wait for some of that lovely French coffee,' says Colette. 'With hot milk, in a bowl.'

'*Au lait* to bed, *au lait* to rise,' says Raffy. 'Hey, that's brilliant. Are you listening? Do you lot get it? It's a three-way pun. English, French and Spanish.'

They all hurry ahead, trying to get away from him. Raffy runs to catch up.

'Where's Didier?' asks Raffy.

'He went home,' says Blanche.

'But why?'

'It happens always,' says Jean-Louis. 'Jean Condom got his father's job, so he thinks he should never socialize with him. He left the party after the dancing started.'

'I'll wake him up when I get home,' says Raffy. 'Tell him not to be a berk.'

'Don't get in beside him,' says Colette. 'Did I tell you that my mum got in beside Jean-Louis?'

Everyone shouts yes. They have all heard this tale several times, but they laugh once again, as Colette insists on going over it.

'This will be me getting into bed at Didier's,' says Raffy, starting to take down his trousers, knowing he has his very best underpants on. 'Making sure I don't get into the wrong bed . . .'

'*Attention!*' shouts Pierre. He has heard another sound coming nearer, though not a roar this time, not another monster from Mars. Instead, a neat little motorbike phut phuts down the street. It stops and Raffy pretends to be a dog, about to relieve himself against it. But the opposite happens. It is the bike which relieves itself, spraying a large jet of water all over Raffy. He shouts in fury, just as a second bike arrives. This one sprays foam over

Raffy, a sweet-smelling deodorant, *aux fleurs*. Oh, how the others all roar.

Blanche can't speak the words to explain that these are further armaments in the war waged by Paris's *Direction de la Propreté*, sent to eliminate all dogshit and make fragrant every nasty corner. Jean-Louis is choking. Pierre is clutching his stomach. The other English kids are holding on to a wall.

Eventually, Raffy gets up from the gutter into which he has fallen under the surprise attack from the spray guns. 'April in Paris,' he sings, slowly swinging round a lamppost, still in his underpants, soaked to the skin but smelling awfully attractive.

Sam: wants to escape

EPISODE 10

SIXTH CENSORED EXCLUSIVE! DIRECT FROM PARIS!
LIZ AINLEY REVEALS ALL

SC: What's the most disgusting thing you've ever done in your bath?

LA: Pull the hairs out of the plughole. They'd been there for ages and I wondered why the water was running away so slowly. The hair was gunged up with slime and horrible sludge and as I pulled it out, it was all matted, in a sort of ball, and it looked just like a dead rat.

SC: Gawd, wish we'd never asked. So what was the most disgusting thing that happened in Paris?

LA: Nothing. It was all lovely, except for Raffy's stupid jokes.

SC: Why did you become a teacher?

LA: Couldn't think of anything else to do. And I thought it would please my mum.

SC: Is your horrible Lancashire accent a handicap when speaking French?

LA: No. No more than Andrew Lloyd Webber's ugly face has affected his writing lovely songs.

SC: How did this French exchange compare with previous ones?

LA: Best so far. But then I say that every year. No, really, it was good. I think nearly everybody got on with their partners, which doesn't often happen. I know I did with mine . . .

SC: If all the down-and-outs in London and Paris could be given homes on condition that you wore the same pair of knickers for ever and ever, would you agree?

LA: Certainly. You never said I couldn't wash them. The knickers, I mean, not the homeless. I'm not sure I could face that.

SC: What presents have you brought home for your husband?

LA: None. He can buy his own.

SC: If Mrs Potter fell under a bus, or even over a bus, would you like to be the Head Teacher of S.T.A.R.S.?

LA: No thanks. Not of anywhere. I couldn't stand the administration. Listening to staff, pupils and parents moaning on all the time – no, thank you. Anyway, I like my subject. Despite the fact that the Government and the Local Education Authorities are doing their best to undermine teachers, especially language teachers. In fact –

SC: That's enough of that stuff. Save it for your memoirs. Hey, little girl, what's your very earliest memory?

LA: Being pushed in a pram, in Liverpool, to watch this boat being launched. It was a very muddy day. I can see it so clearly, all the crowds, the excitement. Yet my mother says she never took me to Liverpool as a baby. I think it's based on a photograph of my sister. Aren't memories funny?

SC: Let us be the judge of that. Talking of judges, your husband is a wealthy QC, whatever that means. Does that mean you would advise girls to marry well?

LA: Are you saying 'Marry, well', or 'Marry well'? To marry, well, that is up to them. Marrying well. Hmm, who can tell how it will all turn out? I happen to be separated, though I don't consider that any of your business.

SC: Do you like frogs' legs?

LA: Watch it. Actually, I'll tell you something interesting. These days, the frogs they eat in France come from India and Pakistan. Their *pâté de foie gras* is likely to come from Israel or Hungary, their truffles from Spain and their snails from China or, wait for it, Britain. The French are a bit sensitive about all this. But French cheese is still French cheese. Camembert and Brie are still home-produced.

SC: Phew, what a relief. Right, in two sentences, how does a hovercraft work? Drawings will gain you no extra marks.

LA: Dunno. I was rotten at science. I suppose it

hovers? Is it on a cushion of air or something? Then it propels itself along? I had to resit O-level Maths and to this day, I don't know how I got through.

SC: Spare us the sob stories. Do the French really like the English?

LA: The ones I know do. They like them very much.

SC: Are you courting? Could a kiss-up situation be about to happen? Is a gigantic snog-in on the way?

LA: Again, it's none of your soddin' business.

SC: Language. What's the rudest French word you know?

LA: *Le rosbif.* That's what the French call an English person, just as we call them Frogs.

SC: Hey, I didn't know that.

LA: You should come to France more often. Or to my French lessons.

School, Monday morning,
sixth-form common room

All the Francophiles, those who exchanged lives and lived to tell the tale, are in high good humour, remembering the good times, boasting about the even better times.

'You wouldn't believe how clean it is,' says Jules, pinning Sam against the wall and refusing to let him go till he at least nods his head to prove that he's been listening.

'Really?' says Sam, trying to cower against the wall, hoping to disappear into the brickwork and not be seen again.

'All week we didn't see any graffiti, no vandalized phone boxes, no litter. Every inch of Paris is clean, but clean. They wash the whole city, every inch of it, every night. Can you believe it? Just ask Raffy . . .'

Jules offers this as a cue for Raffy to jump into gear, ready to start trying to tell Sam once again about this amazing thing which happened to him. Sam is too quick. He slides down the wall and escapes, under feet, under bodies.

'We all became such friends,' says Raffy, turning to shout in Dim's ear, despite Dim's protestations that he is not deaf. 'People changed character. It was amazing. You know how I thought Didier was all posh and stuck-up? Well, in his own home he was a different person, another animal.'

'I've gotta go,' says Dim, pushing his way to freedom.

'You should have seen the *crêpes*,' says Colette to Kirsty. *'Incroyable!'*

'They were so kind,' Taz is saying to Ella. 'Not just our exchanges and their parents, but the ordinary people. In the shops, in the caffs, it was always such good service, compared with horrible old London.'

'Oh,' says Ella. 'So you met ordinary people. That must have been a treat for you.'

'Oh, Ella,' says Taz. 'I didn't mean it that way. Come back, please.'

Everyone has moved away from the Francophiles. Can they be sick of their good times, already bored by all their stories?

'We haven't even told you the best bits yet,'

shouts Raffy. 'My interview with Lizzie was on the level, you know. I did it on the way back, on the hovercraft. All gen stuff. Didn't you think she was good, admitting all that about her husband?'

'Hey, I overheard her in the corridor,' says Colette. 'Her French feller has applied for a job in London! At the Institute of Education.'

'God, is that true?' says Raffy. 'That means that Didier's dad might get his old job back. Did I tell you lot about Didier and his strange dad?'

The couch where Ella and Kirsty were sitting is empty. Dim, Sam and Toby are just about to leave the common room.

'Hold on,' says Colette, grabbing hold of Dim and giving him a big smile. Now that she's back, she can see the virtues in good old Dim more clearly than she ever did before. 'What's the hurry?'

'Nothing,' says Dim, shyly, half-pausing, but not knowing how welcome his presence is.

'Everyone is rushing away,' says Colette. 'Do I smell or something?'

'Actually,' says Toby, very gravely, 'you do. I hate to say it, but –'

'Oh Gawd, it must be this Camembert,' says Colette, holding her *Galeries Lafayette* carrier bag at arm's distance. 'Jean-Louis's grandad gave it to me as a present but my mum won't have it in the house, so I thought I'd give it to Grotty.'

'Lucky old Grotty,' says Sam, standing by the common-room door with Ella. Both of them appear totally uninterested in every detail of the French adventure.

Raffy, Jules, Colette and Taz are beginning to wonder if indeed they ever went to France or if they just dreamt it. Now that they are back in grey, scruffy, predictable, familiar, boring old London, it's as if a screen has dropped, shutting off all that went before.

'Hey, what's happened?' says Raffy, jumping in front of Sam, Toby and Ella.

An idea has suddenly struck him. Could it be not simply that the others have no interest in the French trip, but that something has gone wrong while they've all been away? Something to do with the great condom campaign, perhaps.

'I thought the governors all voted in favour?' says Raffy. 'That's what Dim told me when I rang him up. We were dead chuffed. Had a few vinos to celebrate, I can tell you.'

'They did vote in our favour,' says Toby, 'but Mrs Potter has beaten us.'

'How?' asks Raffy.

'She grassed on us,' says Ella. 'She went straight to a higher body. We had a legal letter first thing this morning from the Education Authority. They own the buildings, the playgrounds, everything. If we were a sixth-form college, like they have in some other London boroughs, it might be different. But we are an all-through school. So, because of the age of our pupils, and all the ethnic backgrounds they come from, the Authority won't allow condoms to be sold on their premises.'

'How about for free, then?' says Raffy. 'You could give them away. Wouldn't that get round it? I'm sure the Tufnell Park Rubber people wouldn't mind doing that, just for the publicity.'

'Raffy,' says Toby, sighing, 'they've beaten us. There's no point in going on.'

'What sickens me,' says Ella, 'is that all through this school they've taught us about freedom, about democracy. For the people, by the people, the rule of law and all that stuff, doing it by the book. Right?'

'Right,' says Raffy.

'So we follow it to the letter,' continues Ella, 'all the way through. We had a free, democratic vote in the Sixth-Form Committee. A free, democratic vote in the governors' meeting. It was carried each time. And where has it got us? Where did it lead? Nowhere. In the end, they fiddled it, they cheated us. So that's it. I'm not taking part in anything in this school ever again.'

'Oh, don't take it like that,' says Colette.

'I can see the point now in being an anarchist,' says Ella. 'Or a dictator. Democracy stinks.'

'You're rushing to extremes,' says Raffy. 'Life is not like that. It's more a matter of compromises, percentages, playing it by ear, fudging, ducking and weaving, making the best of things. In other words, politics.'

'Please don't give up, Ella,' says Jules. 'You've learned something. Next time you'll win, I bet you.'

'You might have lost one battle of the condom,' says Colette, putting her arm round Dim, 'but have you heard about another Condom who is about to fight a different battle? And probably going to win.'

Read the next exciting instalment of the S.T.A.R.S. saga to discover why Toby and Taz are going away together. Can it be true, this dreadful news about Sam's parents? And who is responsible for the Head of Geography's surprising birthday present?

The books in the S.T.A.R.S. series

1. FIT FOR THE SIXTH

A new term, a new life in the sixth form at St Andrews Road School. Enter Jules, the best dressed, Sam, looking serious and trying to stand next to Ella, Colette, the mimic and chocoholic, Dim, looking uncomfortable in his new trainers, Raffy, loud-mouthed as ever and flirting with Kirsty.

2. RAPPING WITH RAFFY

Being rich and famous is what it's all about – at least that's what Raffy thinks. And the way he plans to make it is by being a pop star. Pity he can't sing, dance or play any instruments . . . Ella and her girlfriends decide to ignore his giant ego – the combination of their plans and Raffy's ambitions could be dramatic. Will there be tears and tantrums, or will someone find fame and fortune?

3. SHE'S LEAVING HOME

Colette and her mother are forever arguing. If it's not about Colette's future, it's about her mother's boyfriend. Or her mother's high-heeled shoes. Or her mother's tight jeans. Parents' night at St Andrews Road School makes Colette cringe, but being accused by her mum of pinching money is the last straw.

4. PARTY, PARTY

The sixth form Christmas party has all been planned – the disco, the food, the booze – when it turns out banned. Raffy's fault, of course. He and the football team wrecked the common room, after post-match drinkies with the opposition. But suddenly it's chunky, hunky, clever old Dim who steps up, to make the day, and a bit of money . . .

5. ICE QUEEN

Taz is elegant, exotic and elusive. She's been at S.T.A.R.S. for almost a term now, but still no one knows her, or her secrets. So what a challenge, especially for our Raffy. He knows he's witty and sexy and charming, as he's told everyone. But he can't get this message across to Taz when she won't even talk to him. But he is able to help out with her family troubles and at last he has a chance to start melting the Ice Queen . . .

6. WHEN WILL I BE FAMOUS?

The sixth form is buzzing when a BBC film crew arrives to make a documentary. Who will be in it? Will Raffy interfere? It's no surprise to Jules when they ask him to present it – some people have it, some people don't. But making stars out of S.T.A.R.S. is not what Simon from the BBC has in mind. The National Curriculum and Dim's tuck-shop are much more newsworthy. Kirsty and Colette sulk, Sam is bored. But will Jules be famous?

7. WHO DUNNIT?

It's never dull at S.T.A.R.S. but recently things have been heating up. That's why Toby has come up with his great idea – what S.T.A.R.S. needs is a magazine. But no one else shares his enthusiasm. Raffy thinks it'll be dead boring, Kirsty's too busy to help and Sam's being a wimp. Then an anonymous article is posted through Toby's door and everything is suddenly different.

8. A CASE OF SAM AND ELLA

Ella is worried. She thinks she might be pregnant. What will she tell Sam, what about her parents and her future? Sam is useless, as usual. He is distracted, scared stiff that Vinny, the school yob, is out to get him. Sam doesn't know why. He's never done anything to harm Vinny – or has he? And as for his stomach pains, well, what did he ever do to deserve such agony – and why doesn't anybody believe him? Is he really faking it?

10. PLAYING AWAY

What's got into Taz and Toby? They're holding hands and gazing into each other's eyes . . . in a muddy field in Dorset, of all places. What sparked it off? And what is the connection between Taz and little Fen, the first former who hooks on to Toby and then mysteriously disappears? And as for disappearing, will Sam have to leave London?

11. LET'S STICK TOGETHER

When certain items go missing at St Andrews, the search is on for the culprit. Raffy's been acting suspiciously for some time now and seems a natural choice for questioning. Has he really gone too far this time? What will happen to him? And what will happen to S.T.A.R.S. anyway, if the governors opt out of local education? Will it be the end of St Andrews as we know it?

12. SUMMER DAZE

What's everyone doing for the summer holidays? Lucky Toby and Taz are heading for the sun, but what about the rest of the group? How will they survive without each other? Or will they have to?

EVERY COPY SOLD FIGHTS DRUG ABUSE